An Extreme Journey

An Extreme Journey

The Incredible Adventures of Hawk and Paxie

By Noemi Barrios

MILL CITY PRESS

Mill City Press, Inc.
2301 Lucien Way #415
Maitland, FL 32751
407.339.4217
www.millcitypress.net

Paperback ISBN-13: 978-1-6628-1057-2
Ebook ISBN-13: 978-1-6628-1059-6

Dedicated to

Ivan Dean Hutchison who went to his
glorious home called Heaven on July 11, 2012.
To Lydia Garcia who helped me
start this journey in creating the story.
She also went to her home called Heaven
To The Holy Spirit who guided my hand.

The Characters

Sparrow Families:
Hawk, lives in meadowlarksville attends school and is best friends with Paxie.
Mary, Hawk's mother.
Paxie, Hawk's best friend attends a prestigious school in Meadowlarksville, His parents are **Max and Millie McRight.**
Zechariah Birdfield aka Zeke lives in Crow City and is Choirmaster of Crow City Song Sparrows.
Zelda Birdfield, Zeke's estranged mother.
Mrs. Peckingham, Hawk's school teacher.
Mrs.Twitty, Paxie's school teacher.

Rogue Crows:
Willy, Crow City Chair relocated to Crow City from Meadowlarksville.
Jet, covetous crow secretary to Willy.
Leroy, Willy's comrade in arms resides at Scare Crow park.

Friendly Crows:
Jojo, Mayor of Crow City.
Tom, JoJo's assistant from Hootersville.
Stanley, friendly but gullible jail guard.

Heavenly Creatures:

Nahum, guardian angel

Caleb, guardian angel

Malachi,6-winged Golden Eagle from the third heaven

Judah,6-winged lion from the third heaven

Parrots:

Jake, Hawk's friend from Brazil living with Hawk and his mom.

Paco, the large parrot from Brazil employee at James Feed and Seed

Juan, Paco's friend from Brazil employee at James Feed and Seed.

The Quartet:

Teddy, Georgie, Lenny, and Richey performs with Hawk

The people:

Sarah, the little girl in the hospital beloved friend of Hawk

It's A Bird's World

Our feathered friend's behavior is unique as they have their own times and seasons. A day to them may be shorter or longer depending on what they have planned for that day. Nighttime comes early for these birds and except for night creatures, all birds especially sparrows are safely in their comfy home by nightfall. If you listen closely as you're walking by their homes you can hear them snoring, singing, or talking in their sleep. They are those outrageous early birds that are standing on your window ledge singing in the wee hours of the morning letting you know it's time to get up.

Table of Contents

Chapter One
Nightmare at Scarecrow Park

Dusk was rapidly approaching, adding to the escalating trouble at Scarecrow Park that two fugitive sparrow amigos were experiencing already.

"We must fly faster, Hawk!" Paxie anxiously screamed at his sparrow buddy.

"They're catching up to us," agreed Hawk, hurriedly glancing back and almost losing his balance. Gasping for air, he added, "I don't see them, Paxie."

They had flown to Scarecrow Park together; a place neither had visited before – one they should never have come to.

Nervously, Paxie pointed out, "I told you the park was too far away, Hawk."

"That's true," Hawk admitted, "but, Paxie, you sure made the crows furious by taking their food,"

"Well I had no idea it was their food," protested Paxie, extremely annoyed.

Hawk loved to spend time at city parks just watching people. It was as if he could understand them; their diverse yet strange behaviors, which fascinated him. He had a particular appreciation for picnics, though. It was there that he could count on finding food galore. People always provided the birds an outstanding food crumb feast.

But now, Hawk's idea of fun had become a horrendous nightmare here at Scarecrow Park. Neither one of the two friends had ever flown at this outrageous speed before; especially not for a distance this great. Hawk speedily turned around one more time to see if the crows were still pursuing them.

"Good grief! They're still on our tail, Paxie," exclaimed Hawk. Both birds could hear the raucous cawing from the crows.

"Stop! Stop, you thieving sparrows. You'll be sorry you pillaged our food supply," screamed one furious crow at the top of his lungs. By now, both Hawk and Paxie were out of breath, as well as out of time — as two huge crows were about to **swoop down** on top of them.

Fleeing for their lives, both friends began crying out desperately for help.

"Somebody **please save us**!" Paxie bellowed.

"Help us," echoed Hawk.

The hostile crows resounded with laughter as they beheld the horrified faces of the two **helpless** sparrows.

"What shall we do with them?" Willy inquired of his comrade, Leroy.

"Oh, I can think of a thing or two," mused Leroy.

Unexpectedly, Willy hollered in frightened excitement- "**What is that**?"

Immediately, Leroy responded, "It looks like a huge whirlwind!"

"Look at that – there seems to be a fire in the middle of it. Let's scram out of here," Willy yelled out.

Suddenly, the wind kicked up, like an enormous whirlwind rapidly approaching from the north; a great cloud with raging fire engulfing it with brightness all around; whirling everything and tossing it to and fro. The malevolent crows were being sucked in by this overbearing whirlwind and its infernal cloud storm.

Still attempting to flee for their lives, the crows continued spinning uncontrollably, round and round, until they were flung violently against a large tree trunk, and then rapidly slid to the ground, beak-first, and landing sprawled out in the miry mud.

Hawk and Paxie, on the other hand, had been carried far up into the air, as if transported by a cloud, and had amazingly landed safely on their feet. Unbelievably, they found themselves close to the neighborhood where Paxie lived. In sheer amazement at their well-being and safety, they both voiced their shock in unison: "**What has just happened?**"

Not waiting for the answer, both sparrow amigos hightailed it home, knowing they had some explaining to do.

———

Mary was peering out the window, hoping to see Hawk returning home. Suddenly out of nowhere Hawk appeared, screeching his feet to a stop against their front walkway.

"Hawkie! where have you been? I have been so worried," his mother demanded.

"Mom, don't call me that," protested Hawk.

"Hurry and eat, Hawkie. I'm glad to see that you're not harmed. you know you should not have been out after dusk. There are all kinds of night creatures around once it gets dark. You could have been hurt or killed like your—" Mary ended her sentence abruptly.

"Like Dad? Why don't you tell me what happened to him, Mom?"

"Oh Hawkie, it's too late to talk tonight. We will talk in the morning," Mary answered, trying to put off telling Hawk what had happened to his father.

Millie, Paxie's mom, had permitted Paxie more freedom since his recent birthday. However, she had strictly warned him to always come home before dark, because of the night creatures. These creatures were extremely dangerous to birds. Among them were snakes, bats, owls, and all kinds of nocturnal monsters. Little did the sparrow buddies realize there would be one more added to this list, that in the least would present a challenge: **The Infamous Crows**.

Paxie faced his parents' displeasure.

"We will talk in the morning, son," Max stated in a stern voice.

Chapter Two
A Strange Encounter

Paxie was up at the break of dawn, getting his nice leather backpack, which he had gotten for his birthday, ready for school. He paused to look out the window. The telephone wires were filling up with many of his neighbors, carrying on quite a vivid chatter. This was a gathering place for socializing and catching up on the latest gossip The mourning doves were singing their melancholic songs. Their cooing seemed to convey a profound sadness this morning as one, then another, joined the pitiful choir, revealing an event yet to come.

The mockingbirds had been out and about since five a.m., imitating other birds and being quite noisy and mischievous. Larry and Harry, the twin mocking-birds, were almost as extraordinarily good at mimicking other birds as they were at being troublemakers. Their clownish behavior added chatter and confusion.

Paxie himself was amused by all of this. Still looking out the window, he wondered what it would be like to fly above the telephone wires. These were some of the highest wires in the neighborhood, and Paxie was not allowed to fly up there yet. He imagined flying even beyond the wires, above the highest of clouds.

Moments later, Paxie's thoughts were unexpectedly interrupted by his father's command of, "Paxie, **downstairs!**" He hurriedly flew downstairs, forgetting that his parents had forbidden his flying in the house.

"How many times have I told you not to fly indoors?" Millie inquired.

Not allowed to answer, Paxie immediately turned to his father, who loudly stated, "Son, you broke two cardinal rules yesterday. You were out at dusk and you flew past the boundaries we set for you."

"But, Dad," Paxie started to say.

"Silence, Paxton Lee McRight! Your dad is speaking, and you shouldn't interrupt him," demanded his mother, Millie.

Just then Herbie and Heather, Paxie's siblings walked down the stairs, feathers ruffled and sleepy-eyed. "What's all the commotion?" they asked.

"We're talking with Paxie. You and Heather get ready for school," Mom ordered. "Now, Paxton Lee, you will listen to your father. You have embarrassed us enough already."

The McRights were well-respected sparrows in Meadowlarksville Estates. They had a nice modern birdhouse in this area, known for its beautiful shade trees, numerous water fountains, manicured grass, and a variety of flowers and fragrant rose gardens. Max McRight was a prominent member of his neighborhood Board of Directors. Millie often hosted parties with important socialites. Both parents prided themselves in being members in good standing of their community and respectable parents, as Paxie well knew.

"Paxie, you will be restricted to this neighborhood only, and you won't be allowed to see Hawk anymore," Max commanded.

"But Dad, he's my best friend," Paxie protested

"Not another word, young fellow. Get to school," his father ordered.

Paxie went glumly upstairs to get his backpack. Just then, he heard pecking at the window.

"Hawk!" shouted Paxie, "I'm in deep trouble, and here you are."

"Sorry, buddy. Should I tell your parents it was my fault?" Hawk pleaded.

"No. Just go. I'll see you at the shelter after school," said Paxie.

Hawk flew off. The shelter was the hideout where they would hang out. No one knew about it, but the two of them. More pecking at the window,

"Come on, Paxie!" It was his other two friends, Franky and Figgy.

Paxie opened the window and flew out; something else he wasn't supposed to do. Except for emergencies, everyone was to exit out the front door only. Paxie, Figgie, and Franky went flying off to school together.

———

Hawk and Jake the parrot were playing a game of chase in the front yard of Hawk's house.

"Jake, tell me again about the country you're from; a land filled with fruit trees and all kinds of animals, and where it rains a lot. What about the people; what are they like?" asked Hawk.

Jake, an escapee from a zoo aviary, had landed at Hawk's house looking for food and directions to go back to his country. Hawk made friends with the colorful feathered winged creature and he remained.

Jake was having too much fun to answer. Just then, Mary, Hawk's mother saw Jake flying past her front window. She thought it strange to see a parrot flying freely outdoors. But remembering her poor eyesight, she reconsidered; maybe it wasn't a parrot after all. Jake, however, was delighting in his new freedom. He would fly in circles and Hawk would try to catch up with him, almost out of breath.

"This is fun, Hawk! Let's play Hide and Seek," Jake suggested.

That game would be easy for Hawk because Jake had very colorful feathers, easy to discover; vivid red, radiant yellow, and bright green.

"Okay, start counting, Jake," Hawk said in reply.

Jake quickly flew off to hide. Hawk began searching for the parrot in an area covered with high branches. Looking up directly into the morning sun, Hawk became blinded by its bright rays. Suddenly, he saw him. Instead of finding Jake, Hawk found himself staring into a pair of piercing eyes that seemed to see right through him. Hawk's mouth dropped open with amazement. He had heard of these magnificent creatures called eagles. But never in his life did he expect to be face to face with one.

The stranger's eyes were mysterious. They looked stern, yet there was a definite softness about them. The stranger radiated golden light, his feathers were shimmering in the bright morning sun. He appeared strong and authoritative; commanding respect. Hawk was almost breathless and trembled.

In a whisper, Hawk asked, "Who ... who are you?"

It seemed an eternity before the eagle, Malachi, answered him. "That is not important now. You must find your destiny, Hawk. You have been given a gift from the **Most High**." Immediately, the eagle began to fly; he had six enormous and majestic wings as he soared, almost sweeping Hawk off his feet. Soon, the creature faded completely from sight, into the sky.

Hawk was left awestruck by this magnificent sight that had left him with many unanswered questions. "What could this creature mean? Could it be my imagination? How did he know my name; and who is the **Most High**?"

From the front door, his mother, Mary, yelled out to him, "Hawk, you'll be late for school."

Hawk snapped out of his trance. He picked up his tattered backpack and off he flew, forgetting all about Jake, who was still hiding.

Chapter Three
School Days

The school bell at Meadowlarksville Elementary rang at eight a.m. sharp. Paxie, Frankie, and Figgy filed in together, just in time.

Miss Harriet Twitty was the teacher. She had been at Meadowlarksville Elementary since it first opened twenty years earlier. With her graying hair pulled tightly in a bun at the back of her head, Miss Twitty's eyes seemed to almost pop out from her head. The thick glasses on her face served only to magnify them more. Nothing escaped her vision

"Okay class, it's time to hand in your homework," she pleasantly announced.

"Homework?" Paxie questioned, suddenly conscious that he had forgotten all about it, in the gleeful excitement of going to the park with Hawk. Maybe Miss Twitty wouldn't notice right away, he hoped inwardly.

"Paxie, can you tell me the formula for water?" asked Miss Twitty.

Paxie jumped up from his seat.

"Come on, Paxie, you know; the stuff you drink," Miss Twitty prompted. There was a roar of laughter from the class. "All right class, hush now," the teacher admonished.

Paxie felt his mouth dry and his brow sweating. "Well, uh…" he said hesitantly.

"Sit down, I'll see you after school. I have already spoken with your mother," Miss Twittty said dryly. Miss Twitty and Millie McRight, Paxie's mom, belonged to the same bridge club, making it almost impossible for Paxie to get away with much of anything.

Paxie couldn't understand why he needed to study chemistry; but he did know it was one of the requirements for prep school entry, where his parents so wanted him to attend. Formulas were hard for Paxie; in fact, everything seemed hard for him, lately.

———

All-day, Hawk had problems concentrating in class. The only thing he could think of was the eagle that had unexpectedly appeared to him, earlier. In his wonderment, the questions arose again. "What was his name? And what did he mean by 'Find your destiny'? How did he know my name? What gift was the eagle talking about?"

Hawk had seen eagles before, in pictures, but never one like this. This creature was huge. His feathers were shimmering from a golden light that enveloped him. He also had six wings. There was an aura about this winged creature that was unlike anything in this world.

"Where did he come from?" Hawk whispered to himself.

"Are you okay today, Hawk?" asked Miss Peckingham, interrupting his thoughts. "You don't seem like yourself."

'Confused' might have been a more accurate way to describe Hawk. He had not even realized that the school bell had rung, as he continued to sit in the classroom; all alone now.

"I'm fine, Miss Peckingham; just didn't get enough sleep last night, that's all," Hawk noted.

Miss Peckingham had a kind and gentle nature. She was fond of Hawk and was friends with the student's mother, Mary. As his teacher, she was well aware of the young student's potential. He certainly had a gift for singing and sang some of the most beautiful songs ever heard; songs that warmed one's heart.

"Where did you learn those songs?" she would inquire.

They seemed to emanate from a sensitive, loving heart. They radiated peace to all who heard them. Hawk was shy by nature and had only one true friend, whom Miss Peckingham knew attended a different school. Recently, his teacher had seen Hawk hanging around with a parrot named Jake, but where Jake came from, she didn't know.

Going back to her previous conversation with him, Miss Peckingham stated, "Your mother was worried about you being out after dusk yesterday, Hawk,"

"I know. I just wanted to see the people, again," said Hawk.

Miss Peckingham quickly responded with concern, "You need to be careful, Hawk. Not all people are friendly."

With that, Hawk immediately spotted an opportunity to inquire about what was uppermost in his mind. He grasped the moment to ask, "Miss Peckingham, do you know what happened to my father?"

Miss Peckingham looked at him sadly and stated, "Hawk, your mother loves you very much and is protecting you. She will tell you at the right time."

Disappointed with her reply, but more determined than ever, Hawk made up his mind he would find out the truth that very evening.

———

However, Paxie was not having it so easily at his school.

"Paxie, you're a bright bird. Why have you been so troubled lately?" Miss Twitty asked, "Your mother has been troubled ever since you have been hanging around with Hawk, and your grades have been going downhill. He's not your kind, Paxie. Keep in mind that you will be going to a prestigious school someday, and you are an 'A' student with a great future ahead of you."

"Hawk's my friend, Miss Twitty," retorted Paxie. "And Hawk is very smart. He's just poor. He used to attend this school, remember?" Paxie continued.

"Used to, Paxie. He's not with us any longer," Miss Twitty emphasized. "You'd better go home, now."

Paxie flew off, but not toward his house.

Chapter Four

The Incident At The Hideout

There was a wooded place near the school, with a small creek that flowed downhill into a small pond. Hawk would frequently hide out in that area to think, but it was also a play and fun place for him. It was a secret haven for him and his friend, Paxie.

Raindrops were beginning to fall. Hawk was looking at his reflection in the small pond as his thoughts went back to the eagle and lingered on the large bird's words to him. Hawk did not hear Paxie arrive.

Jumping almost a foot in the air, Hawk exclaimed, "Hey, Paxie, you scared me."

"I was sure you would be here, Hawk, and I wanted to talk with you," replied Paxie in a serious-sounding voice.

"I have something to tell you, too, Paxie," answered Hawk.

"Hawk, my parents aren't going to let me hang out with you anymore," blurted Paxie, his voice broken, sad with emotion, and tears filling his eyes.

"Oh, how I will miss you, Paxie! You've been such a good buddy to me," replied Hawk, clearly shaken and crying.

"This isn't fair," Paxie burst out; "What are we going to do?"

"Paxie, I'm leaving. I need to find out something. I need answers to many questions." It was then that Hawk shared with Paxie about his encounter with the golden eagle and what the eagle told him about having a destiny from the Most High. As Hawk described Malachi, Paxie listened wide-eyed and intent.

Eagles are respected creatures, thought Paxie, *but this one sounds most extraordinary.* Paxie sensed that Hawk had many things to search out. *Was this for real?* pondered Paxie.

"Destiny, huh? Well, I will go with you, and maybe I can find mine, too," was Paxie's comical reaction. "I'm tired of all my parents' restrictions on me, anyhow."

"No, no, Paxie, I don't think you should be going with me..." Hawk said pensively.

Interrupting Hawk abruptly, Paxie stated, "I'm going anyway!"

"Hush for a moment, Paxie. Do you hear that?" Hawk interjected.

"Hear what?" Paxie asked.

Hawk sensed they were being watched. He thought he heard the rustling of feathers and the sound of very large footsteps. Maybe it was the wind. The creek was gurgling. It was beginning to thunder, and lightning lit up the now dusky sky. The two became silent momentarily, attuned only to the sound of raindrops

Paxie broke the silence. "I've always wondered what's out there, too, Hawk. My parents barely let me go beyond my neighborhood."

Hawk's emotions were evoked as his mind pictured new places and people. "I've always wondered what it's like to fly high up in the clouds," he said in amazement.

"Ever wonder what they're made of, Hawk?" questioned Paxie, looking skyward.

Both friends were very excited and started giggling with anticipation. Unexpectedly, they heard the sound of what they presumed to be heavy footsteps. Alarmed, Hawk turned toward the direction of the sound.

"Stay here, Paxie. I'm going to take a look. Maybe I can see something out there," said Hawk in a half-whisper.

Hawk flew into a thicket of bushes and trees. As the thunder and lightning continued heavily, storm clouds darkened the sky like a canopy. A loud, deafening crack of thunder, accompanied by a bright flash of lightning, suddenly split a tree from top to bottom. Thick smoke billowed from its trunk. At the exact moment the lightning illuminated the sky, Hawk saw a huge person with immense wings. He seemed to be twenty feet tall, and was engulfed in fire. The fire surrounded him but did not burn him. He was dressed in white and sparkled with radiance. The fire appeared as liquid flames churning around and through the person. His eyes, also, were brilliant with a fiery glow. In his right hand, he carried a long sword that gleamed with the fire's reflection.

Hawk was stunned and frightened by the sight. He had the impulse to take flight, as fast as possible. Instead, he remained motionless, stiff, as if glued to the branch he stood on. Never had he witnessed anything as enormous as this broad-winged being. Then just as rapidly as he appeared, the being vanished.

"Don't be afraid," a voice uttered, "he's not a human; he's an angel."

Somehow, this seemed a familiar voice, and Hawk turned at the sound of it, gazing in surprise at the eagle he had met that morning.

"What a strange situation; first an angel, and now this strange golden eagle again," mumbled Hawk within. Bewildered by it all, Hawk felt as if he would faint.

"I'm Malachi, from the Third Heaven," voiced the eagle. "You, Hawk, have been given a gift to see many things. You have a journey ahead of you," the eagle proclaimed.

Hawk remained silent and in awe.

"Just remember, things are not always what they appear to be," warned Malachi. "You must learn to '*see*' with your heart," the golden six-winged eagle instructed. With that, Malachi was gone, like a flash of lightning.

Hawk was left trembling and speechless. He twirled around to fly off. Paxie, tired of waiting, had just landed close behind him, but missed the heavenly display and all. Hawk flew right into him.

"Owww, Hawk!" screamed Paxie. "Why don't you watch where you're going?"

"Paxie," responded Hawk with a shrill, "you'll never believe what I just saw!"

"Hawk, it's already dark and Mom and Dad will surely kill me, this time. I'll be grounded forever." Pausing briefly, Paxie asked, "What's wrong with you, Hawk? You look pale."

"Paxie, I saw him again," yelled Hawk at the top of his voice. "I saw the eagle, Malachi. And I saw a gigantic human too, with wings like us, but his wings were **huge**. Malachi said it was an **angel,**" cried Hawk, talking so fast, he never heard a word Paxie had said.

"Hawk! Later! I've got to go. **Let's both get out of here, now**," yelled Paxie. He grabbed Hawk by the shirt and off they flew. Paxie wanted to hear all that Hawk had to say, but the thought of his parents' furious reaction upon his arrival home made him choose otherwise.

Chapter Five

The White Feather

J ake was in the small living room of Mary and Hawk's home, enjoying a cup of tea with her. They were having a conversation about Jake's awful experience in the zoo's aviary.

"Yes, Ms. Mary," Jake remembered, "it was like being in prison."

"You poor dear," lamented Hawk's mother. "How tragic it must have been. After all, Jake, you had been flying freely in extensive forests adorned with beautiful flowers, alive with winding rivers, and such. And to be locked up with birds you didn't even know…" Mary commented.

"But now I have you and Hawk as friends," exclaimed Jake.

"Yes Jake, we love your company," stated Mary. She wondered out loud, "Where is Hawk, anyway?" She realized she had lost track of time as she conversed with Jake. "Here it is late again, and he's out there in a thunderstorm. Oh, I hope he's not in danger," she stated anxiously.

As if by magic, Hawk walked in the front door at precisely that moment. He was dripping wet, carrying his equally soaked backpack.

"Hawkie! Where have you been? Look at you; you're drenched," his mother scolded. "You'll probably catch a cold, too," she added. Looking more closely at her son, Mary asked preoccupied, "What's wrong? You look as if you've seen a ghost."

"No, Mom, not a ghost, but a... Oh, never mind," was Hawk's automatic response. Turning to Jake, he greeted, "Hi, Jake," and swiftly made a beeline to his room, slamming the door shut as he entered.

Jake said his good-byes to Hawk's mother and left promptly. Jake spent his nights in the trees, never wanting to be confined to a house. Since his experience at the aviary, Jake often awakened with nightmares about being imprisoned in restrictive places.

Mary hastened to Hawk's undersized bedroom and knocked urgently on his door.

"Yes, Mom?" was Hawk's immediate reaction.

"I want to talk to you, Hawkie," his mom advised. "You seem disturbed about something. I'm worried because you were out too late tonight, and it was storming terribly. What on earth were you doing in this weather? I spoke with Miss Peckingham today;

she's troubled about you, too. You asked her about your father?" Mary inquired.

"Yes, Mom. I want to know what happened to him. Tell me now, please. I must know!" insisted Hawk.

"Yes, Hawkie, I understand. I, too, think it's time for you to know."

Hawk's mother sat next to her son on his bed and began, "It's been a long time, but even so, it's still difficult for me to talk about it. It was late one summer eve, and the sun was beginning to set. We were coming back from a party, your father, Uncle James, and I.

"We stopped to rest on the wall of a nearby city named Hootersville. From our position, we could see a beautiful water fountain cascading its water into a small pond. We thought the cool water would be refreshing after our long, tiresome flight. We alighted on the pond and all three of us at one time, began taking our drink."

Mary paused to take a deep breath and continued once more. "I saw it first – a frightful sight! A dead sparrow was floating on the pond. I knew immediately something was wrong. Before I could say anything, a rock came whirling past me with forceful speed and hit your father in the chest. He fell instantly into the water." Mary started to sob with great sadness. "As I looked on in shock, I could see his blood tinting the water. That image still haunts me to this day."

As Hawk listened attentively, Mary went on. "In a great panic, your uncle James flew in one direction, and

I in another. I perched myself on an out-of-the-way tree to see what would happen next. I saw two very large boys run toward the fountain. One was swinging a piece of wood shaped like a 'Y'. Then I heard a piercing scream. A little girl ran toward the fountain, along with her mother, and the boys speedily escaped from the scene. The little girl was crying. As I saw her, I realized that in my shock and turmoil, I was unable to cry."

Mary proceeded, "I looked up at James, who was saying, 'We need to go, Mary. We could be in danger.' But I told him, 'No! I can't leave Jonah like this.' Then I saw the little girl's mother gently pick up your father and the other bird out of the water. They went into their house for what seemed an eternity. When they finally emerged, they had with them two small boxes."

Pausing in her conversation, Mary noticed that Hawk was crying. "Oh, Hawkie," she said voicing compassion. "I knew this would be hard for you," she continued, "The mother and the little girl buried both your dad and the other bird in their yard, under a rose-bush. Every year about this time, I go back and visit the gravesite."

Hawk was angry, confused; but most of all deeply saddened. Why had they done this to his father? Hawk always found people to be interesting and charming. He could even understand what they were saying. This repulsive action shocked him, but he also felt hatred stirring in his heart.

As Mary looked at him, it seemed that Hawk's eyes, which normally were bright and kind, appeared darkened. She was startled even more when she heard him say, "I hate these people, Mom. I wish they were dead!"

"Hawkie! You can't mean that," Mary expressed loudly.

"Yes, I do," screamed Hawk.

"But remember this, Hawkie; there are good people and there are bad ones. The mother and little girl were good persons," Mary pointed out to her hurting son.

Hawk, however, would hear none of this. It seemed his whole world was now turned upside down. Hadn't Miss Peckingham warned him earlier at school, today, that not all people were friendly? Now he would never trust humans.

Mary left the room shortly and then returned with a little wooden box. "I've been saving this for you, Hawkie," she said as she opened the box. It was a white feather. "This was your dad's. I went early the next day to the pond, despite James's advice not to. I saw the little girl playing in her front yard. My eyes fell on this white feather on the ground. I knew immediately it was your dad's. I flew down to scoop it up and my eyes met the young girl's. She stood looking at me for a few seconds. It was almost as if she recognized me. She smiled, and then I flew away."

Hawk gently took the silky white feather, holding it close to his breast. Thoughts, deep and sorrowful, filled his heart as he felt its smooth texture. Then anger abruptly took over his emotions, recalling again the horrendous abomination that had taken his father's life. Hawk had completely forgotten about Malachi and the angel he had seen.

Hawk still held fast to the precious white feather while his mother went into her minute kitchen to make some tea. As he thought lovingly of his dad, Hawk longed to see him; to be with him. But the impossibility of it caused him to despair. His thinking then turned to vengeance. The hopelessness of achieving his desire drove him to melancholy and frustration.

How can I possibly avenge my father? wondered Hawk, his heart burning with hostility. "Oh, there must be some way," he said, seeking to contrive a plan in his mind, yet sobbing with pain.

Mary filled her cup with the warm tea and prepared a cup for Hawk also. Usually, she didn't let him drink tea, but today was different, so she made an exception. She put a little honey in the cup and took it to Hawk. Entering his room, she called to him encouragingly, "Hawkie, here's some warm tea for you."

Hawk did not answer. He had fallen asleep with the white feather by his side. Mary perceived the ache in her son's heart and how dear his father was to him.

She too went to bed finally, finding sleep only after hours of concern for her offspring. Besides her aging parents, Hawk was all Mary had left in life, and he was precious to her.

Chapter Six
Darkness To Light

Hawk woke up earlier than usual the next morning. It was still dark outside. Packing his backpack with what he thought he would need for a long journey, he was careful not to awaken his mother. She would strongly object to his leaving. Peeking into his mother's bedroom, he stared at her for a lengthy time, deciding if he should leave her. Revenge and sadness assailed him, holding his thoughts captive, adding to the misery of making a choice.

"Good-bye, Mother, I have to do this," he whispered. Picking up his backpack, he gently placed the wooden box with his father's white feather inside it.

Hawk closed the front door and flew past Jake. He was perched on a branch where he now lived.

"Good-bye, ole' friend, I know we'll meet up again soon."

"Nice to meet you too," mumbled Jake, talking in his sleep.

There was a cool breeze in the early morning air. Hawk noticed a large star shimmering unusually against a blue-black velvety sky. Hawk thought he heard music coming from the star's distant location.

"That's odd, I never noticed that before."

He shook it off thinking he was still half asleep. Maybe it was Jake's wind chimes that he had placed on a branch, to make his new place more like a home; a gift from Mary.

How thoughtful and sweet of my mother, he pondered, with tears in his eyes, adding to the difficulty of leaving her.

Hawk flew out of his neighborhood and through the city of Meadowlarksville, which sat in a valley. The sun was now beginning to peek over the hills, few city lights were on and the sky was beginning to fill up with a variety of birds. Flying to their daily jobs and scheduled appointments, many groups of winged creatures traveled together with their backpacks, lunch pails, and briefcases. Some even had hard hats on.

Hawk flew past a group of mourning doves. Their melancholic sounds echoed in the early morning air.

They sound sorrowful, thought Hawk. "Well I have enough problems of my own," exclaimed Hawk.

"Don't we all!" yelled out one of the doves flying past Hawk.

"Oh, I didn't see you," apologized Hawk.

The dove didn't answer. Picking up speed, he called out to the group of doves, "Wait up, my alarm didn't go off!"

Returning his attention to vengeful thoughts, Hawk picked up speed, remembering the distance to Hootersville. He did not want to be out in the dark. He would stop in Hootersville briefly to find his father's grave, then continue to Crow City, hoping to get answers. Thinking of his father's grave saddened him. His thoughts quickly gave in to vengeful, angry thoughts. So focused was Hawk on thoughts of getting even, he didn't realize how dark it had become.

"Oh my, a storm is coming."

But there were no signs of a storm approaching, just an increase of darkness.

"How can this be?" asked Hawk. "I do not see a storm."

Flying faster, he continued to meditate on vengeful thoughts. The angrier he became, the darker it became. Hawk could fly no further. He perched on a branch. It was now pitch dark.

"What is happening, why is it so dark? I can't see!" Frightened by this strange event, Hawk started to cry.

Suddenly two glowing lights flew by him. "Brighten your life! Brighten your life, you are in the dark!" It was two of the doves Hawk saw earlier. They were glowing like lamps and had no problems flying.

"How do I do that?" asked Hawk. "Hey, come back, tell me how to brighten my life," he yelled out, but he got no answer. The doves' lights became dimmer and dimmer as they flew away.

Peculiar noises surrounded him. Howling and screeching from some unknown thing terrified him.

"Oh, this is scary, I want to go home," said Hawk. He started to cry again and stopped abruptly on hearing the rustling of feathers. Holding his breath, Hawk could feel his heart pounding.

Turning quickly, he saw two huge round yellow eyes staring at him.

"What are you doing here, little bird?" an owl said from the dark. "Don't you know It's dangerous out here?"

"Yyyyess...." Hawk stuttered, "but I can't see. It's too dark."

Staring at Hawk with suspicion, the owl finally said, "Well, maybe I can help you."

Hawk welcomed the help, but then remembered what his mother told him about nocturnal creatures such as owls. He noticed more scary eyes around him and even saw sharp teeth.

"Well, I uh. I uh will be okay," said Hawk, backing away from the owl. The owl lifted his wings and flew away. Relieved, Hawk sighed, "Oh, that was a close one." However, the howling screeching and now growling continued. It was more than Hawk could bear.

"You better hide," squeaked a tiny voice behind Hawk.

He turned around to see where the voice came from.

The tiny voice continued, "You are lucky that owl didn't have you for his dinner."

Hawk saw the speaker was a mouse, and was about to say something, but instantaneously the mouse ran away.

"Wait, come back!" He wondered why the little visitor ran away so suddenly.

Hawk didn't see the owl flying swiftly toward him with wings spread out and large talons aimed in his direction until it was too late. The scared little sparrow knew what was coming. Closing his eyes, he shook violently. Thoughts of his mom and dad flashed through his mind. He would miss Paxie. Hawk sighed, with tears in his closed eyes, waiting for the end.

Closing in toward his prey, the owl's strong talons would crush his little body in one swift movement. Suddenly.... **swoop**! Hawk felt the wind across his face and the brushing of wings across his head. He also heard the whirring of huge wings. With his eyes still shut, Hawk trembled.

"Open your eyes, Hawk," commanded a familiar voice. Hawk sensed light around him again. The authoritative voice commanded again: "Open your eyes, Hawk."

Hawk opened his eyes. The light was all around him.

With the flash of his enormous wings, Malachi repelled the darkness. **It was gone**. Hawk was speechless, but he was still trembling. The owl and ter-rifying noises had vanished, and most importantly, the dark was now light.

"Darkness has to flee in the presence of light, Hawk," declared Malachi.

Flabbergasted, Hawk stared at Malachi and the doves. A peace enveloped him. He felt so much lighter.

"Brighten your life," exclaimed one of the doves,

"Yes, brighten your life," quipped another dove.

"Your vengeful thoughts darkened your heart," said Malachi.

"Your lamp was going out," exclaimed one of the doves.

"You mean there was no darkness except in my mind?" asked Hawk.

"In your heart," stated Malachi. He continued, "Your vision was blinded by dark vengeful thoughts. Stay in the light. You will have to learn to see with your heart, too. Remember, you have a destiny from the Most High." With that stated, Malachi and the others disap-peared, leaving Hawk to ponder whether they all had really appeared to him at his most dismal hour.

Hawk looked up to the sky, where shimmering gold feathers were falling, a display of the visitor's confir-mation. Hawk felt so peaceful.

Chapter Seven
Left Behind

What a journey this will surely be! Hawk imagined. He'd hardly made it past the Meadowlarksville city limits and already he was awestruck by the events that had just taken place. Fortunately, the atmosphere had cleared now, and Hawk could fly with ease once again. He glided over grassy fields; terrain void of everything but dirt, and stretches of paved surfaces; all the while contemplating all that had occurred only hours ago.

"I don't know what destiny Malachi is talking about," considered Hawk loudly, "but I certainly have my own quest. What does he mean by my vision being blinded by dark thoughts?" Hawk questioned. "I can see perfectly fine. I've never seen more clearly than I do now."

———

It was a cloudy day, and the lunch bell at Meadowlarksville Elementary School had just resounded. Paxie ran out of his classroom to catch up with Figgy. He needed lunch money. Since his father, Max, had placed him on restriction and cut off his allowance, he could only have his lunch money, but Paxie had spent his lunch money unwisely.

"Come on, Figgy! I'll pay you back soon, and with interest," pleaded Paxie.

Incidentally, Figgy was called by that name because he loved to eat figs and continually had the remnants of them on his beak.

"You're the only friend I've got now, Figgy," Paxie emphasized as he pressured his schoolmate. Paxie had been shunned by his friends; those whose parents were well acquainted with his mom and dad. These individuals avoided him because Paxie was repeatedly in trouble, due to his relationship with Hawk. However, the two had parted a few days before, when Hawk left to an unknown destination to find his father's murderers.

Figgy took pity on Paxie and bought him lunch. Both Paxie and Figgy bought their food from the school cafeteria, then went outdoors to a wooden picnic table to eat.

"You're foolish, Pax, to hang around Hawk," remarked Figgy. "No one around here likes outsiders."

"But Figgy, Hawk used to come to this school also; just a year ago, even," protested Paxie, in defense of Hawk.

Within minutes, Figgy's classmates Frankie and Jack, two popular sparrows, flew to the table Paxie and

Figgy were at. As soon as they saw Paxie, though, both visitors left.

"See what I mean?" Admonished Figgy.

Sighing deeply, Paxie was convinced that life was against him, for reasons beyond his understanding. He had lost his best friend, Hawk, his parents were quite displeased with him, and Miss Twitty seemed to always be on his tail. Now on top of all that, Paxie wasn't even sure of Figgy's friendship anymore.

"I'll have to go talk to Frank, Pax. I'll see you later," stated Figgy, somewhat reluctantly.

"Do whatever, Fig," mumbled Paxie in return.

Figgy winged over to Frankie and Jack's table, far away from Paxie. A drizzle was beginning to cover the gray and dismal atmosphere; a reflection of what Paxie felt in his heart, it seemed.

"Oh, where could Hawk be?" wondered Paxie. "I miss him already."

The raindrops were getting bigger, as Paxie sat there, feeling all alone in the world. With emotions frayed and dejected, Paxie began to weep softly. He couldn't bring himself to eat his lunch and left it for the ants to feast on it.

—

Meanwhile, over distant skies, Hawk finally arrived at Hootersville. He had made a wrong turn earlier and ended up in a different town named Wren City. Having become consumed with grievous imaginations, Hawk had missed the turnoff to Hootersville.

As he fluttered his way to his dad's gravesite, Hawk felt a cloud of anxiety hover over him. He stopped at a park and perched himself on a wooden table. Taking his lunch of mixed seed and bread from his backpack, Hawk meditatively began to eat. His thoughts took him back to his friend Paxie, wondering what he could be doing at this time. Then his mother, Mary came to mind.

"She would probably be thinking I'm in school right now," Hawk surmised, "until she reads my letter." In his letter, Hawk had said his good-bye to his mom, not mentioning his true intention, to avoid upsetting her. He had written it in large letters, recalling it was difficult for her to read the small print.

A group of people having a picnic prompted Hawk to leave the area, lunch unfinished. He didn't want to observe or be too close to people, yet. He had not over-come his suspicion of them after hearing of his father's violent demise. He certainly didn't intend to wait around to find out the outcome of his visit there, although these individuals seemed cheerful enough. He also noticed that the atmosphere around them was pleasant, and it puzzled him that they prayed before taking their meal. He did not know what that meant.

It was late afternoon when Hawk found the house his mother had described. He saw the cascading fountain and the beautifully landscaped yard. Before him was the rose garden with many colorful flowers, as Mom had mentioned. Hawk was beset with mixed emotions of fear and anxiety. He feared not knowing if those "murderers" were still around. At this point, he didn't feel quite so bold. Atop a tree branch, surveying the area, Hawk saw the rosebush where his mom said his beloved dad was laid to rest.

Chapter Eight
Double Rainbows and Best Friends

Paxie decided he would go to the hideout after school. *Maybe Hawk didn't leave after all. Maybe he changed his mind and he could be at the creek where we love to hang out,* Paxie thought wistfully, his hopes rising. He could make it over there in a jiffy before his parents got home. He remembered they would be at some high society retreat all day, at the country club. He also remembered their harsh warnings of the disciplinary measures they would take, should he fail to follow their instructions.

Paxie flew to the wooded area where the two friends always met and landed on a rock near the creek.

"I'll wait here for a short while; maybe he's late from school," Paxie reasoned.

As customary for the season, the rain began to fall once more and Paxie watched the raindrops descend into the creek. His mind revisited the scene of the last time he and Hawk had spent time together here, and he started to weep.

"Hawk said he had seen an angel. What could that be? And the eagle named Malachi; who was he?" All these questions whirled around in his mind, as Paxie thought out loud of what Hawk had related to him. "Hawk has been acting strange lately," Paxie uttered to himself. Wrapped up in those images, he stood, unaware that an angel of great stature stood beside him. The angel was clothed in white, with a gold sash around his chest.

———

Back in Hootersville, Hawk remained looking at the red rose bush and the small grave with a white cross where his father lay. He trembled as tears streamed down his face. Flying down to the foot of the gravesite, Hawk could feel the moisture on his back, as the clouds broke forth with light rain.

Hawk had never really known his father. He had few memories of him, since he was so young when his father died, and now the opportunity to know him was gone. The feeling of loss and pain tore at his heart. He missed his father so. Hawk took out the white feather he had in his backpack, handling it with gentle care; the last treasured reminder of his dad.

Hawk stood at the grave for a long period, weeping profoundly and almost uncontrollably. When he gained his composure, he noticed that the rain had stopped. He also became aware of a sense of peace and consolation that came over him. Something very odd was happening, he noticed. Small white feathers, the purest of white, were cascading down from the sky and falling all around him.

"What on earth is this?" he inquired in an audible voice. Rubbing his eyes, Hawk looked upward. "Maybe this is snow? No! These are feathers; it's raining tiny white feathers all over! How incredible." Hawk watched in astonishment. He was entirely awed by the rainfall of feathers; fine silky feathers tumbling downward everywhere. The feather shower began to slacken moments later, finally coming to an end.

Still contemplating the sky, Hawk then noticed two beautiful rainbows that had suddenly appeared from nowhere.

"Oh my," Hawk exclaimed. "I've never seen such vibrant colors. Double rainbows, side by side, like two best friends." Instantly he was reminded of his special friend, Paxie; his genuine buddy.

By now the sky had cleared and had become a beautiful blue, hovering over the earth. Appreciating the beauty of the sky and the events that had just occurred, Hawk had momentarily forgotten his insatiable anger. He glanced back at his father's grave, bidding his cherished parent farewell. Then he tucked the feather in his backpack and took to the air.

As he distanced himself from that city, Hawk felt he should head north. He had heard his mother talk about the City of the Crows aka Crow City. Maybe there he would find who he was searching for? Hawk wondered in his heart. With that thought, Hawk pursued his north-ward destination.

———

In the meantime, Paxie found himself alone once again, and sorely missing his dear friend, Hawk, over-come by weeping again. But his conscience was telling him he would soon have to go home and face his par-ents. Wanting to avoid the encounter, Paxie began to think of running away to find Hawk.

Looking to the sky as if for answers, Paxie observed that the rain had refrained from falling, but in place of it, two beautiful rainbows appeared, as if they had been painted in the sky. Double rainbows, of deep pur-plish-blue, red and yellow; so vibrant. There was even an emerald green shade. Paxie had never seen such a stunning, breathtaking sight before. Two rainbows, side by side, like two best friends

Chapter Nine

Crow City

Sundown was approaching when Hawk flew into the City of the Crows. Earlier, he had stopped briefly on the outskirts of the town, resting on the city limits sign.

All at once, Hawk saw two mockingbirds soaring at high speed toward him, as if being pursued. They slowed down when they got to Hawk.

One yelled out, "Buddy, you don't want to stop at this place!"

The other called out, "C'mon, Henry! before they catch up to us." Then they headed out of the city, flapping their wings ferociously.

Hawk kept his eye on them until all he could see was two dark specks in the horizon.

"They must have been desperate to escape from this town before evening," Hawk surmised He wondered who could be chasing them.

The incident over, Hawk immediately turned his attention toward finding a place to turn in for the night. He did not want to be out at dusk and this was an unfamiliar place. After his encounter with the two strangers from this town, also known as Crow City, Hawk thought it wise to be cautious.

There was a mad rush in the city sky as many of the birds were trying to get to their final destination for the night. A dove almost flew into Hawk at high velocity, shrieking as it passed, "For crying out loud, watch where you're going, you silly bird."

"Me?" responded Hawk, alarmed. "We would have been 'squashed ducks' had we collided." Taking a deep breath, Hawk regained calmness.

Crow City certainly was noisy. Not only was there heavy traffic in the skies, but the streets were congested with trucks and cars honking, screeching their brakes, and disturbingly loud engines. The smell of exhaust filled the air, causing Hawk to cough and almost choke from it.

"I'd better get some water," Hawk decided. He flew into Crow Municipal Park just in time, the sky almost in darkness. The park seemed like a small sanctuary amidst the city's chaos. Sighting a water fountain nearby, Hawk fluttered his way to it, only to find it dry.

Feeling uneasy, Hawk froze for a moment. He sensed many eyes staring at him. Turning around with unusual quickness, he saw nothing. Then he spotted a small pond and flew to it to take a fast drink. After that, he continued to a nearby pine tree. As he made his way there, he was confronted face to face by an extraordinarily large black crow.

"There's no room, here. Find your own place, sparrow!" bellowed the unfriendly crow. This stirred a commotion among the other crows in the tree.

"Yeah, get out of here!" hollered another. "No sparrows allowed!"

Still, another screamed, "Who does he think he is?"

Hawk abandoned the pine tree and went to another. Faced with more crows, the tired sparrow yelled in frustration, "Rats! Crows everywhere. And it's already dark. What am I going to do now?"

He considered he might have to leave the park, but unexpectedly he heard a voice that came from behind him. "Hey, Buddy. You're not going to find a place to sleep tonight that easy. You must be new to Crow City."

Turning his head, Hawk saw another sparrow, just like him. The bird was swinging from a tree limb, hanging upside down. Rapidly, the sparrow turned himself right side up, announcing, "Name's Zeke. What's yours?" Zeke was a larger than average sparrow. He wore a patch over his right eye and a red bandana around his neck.

"Why, it's Hawk," he stated. "And what were you doing, hanging upside down from the tree limb?"

"Oh, that?" Zeke responded. "Just wanted to see what it was that bats see in it. A different view, anyway."

"Ugh! Bats," Hawk said, disgusted. "They're creepy." His response stemmed from the many negative stories he had heard about bats, as a youngster.

"Shhhh," Zeke warned. "There's a bunch that hangs around here. Crows don't like them either."

"There are lots of crows here," observed Hawk.

Zeke laughed with unrestraint.

"What's so funny?" Hawk was curious to know.

"Crow City, my friend. It's their city," Zeke squawked emphatically.

"I need to find a place to spend the night," bemoaned Hawk.

"Ah, yes," said Zeke. "Let me see what I can do for you. Come with me," he instructed Hawk, winging his way to a gigantic oak tree. Hawk followed behind. The oak tree was teeming with birds of all kinds, seeking shelter for the night. Zeke spoke to a crow that was in charge of the place.

"Okay, just one night and that's it, Zeke. This isn't a hotel for just anyone. And he needs to be gone by the crack of dawn," the crow, named JoJo, informed the large sparrow.

"Fair enough," Zeke conceded. "Come on, Hawk."

So Hawk spent his first night away from home in the huge oak tree crowded with all species of birds. He perched himself next to Zeke. The accommodations were not very comfortable for Hawk. He was used to his own room, in a comfy house. During the night, some birds were snoring, while others even sang in their sleep. Perhaps tomorrow things would be different, Hawk hoped. He was too tired to think anymore and before long, he dozed off, fast asleep.

ChapterTen
Rude Awakening

Hawk woke up at the crack of dawn, to the sound of noisy confusion in the air. He could hear the crows caw-cawing above him. Several of them were engaged in a contentious fight over food.

"Where am I?" Hawk loudly questioned.

He had just said this when Zeke yelled to him, "Get down!"

A flying acorn scarcely missed Hawk's head.

"Come on, Hawk," insisted Zeke. "Let's get out of here. The crows are up in a frenzy this morning; someone stole their stash of food."

Hawk started to pick up his backpack when out of nowhere, a giant black crow tried to grab it from him.

"Let me see what you've got there, sparrow," demanded Willy, a bossy crow.

"Ah, come on, Willy, he's new here. He doesn't know the rules yet," Zeke explained, hoping to deter the demanding crow.

Hawk was still holding on to his backpack when he suddenly remembered that he had placed his father's white feather in it.

Willy, forcefully opposing the sparrow, yanked the backpack open, nearly tearing the flap off. "Well, what have we here?" remarked Willy in triumph.

"Give me that back," shouted Hawk in protest.

"Hey, fellows, look. A white feather," Willy boasted. "Bud, this will look good in your hat.

"No, It won't," Jojo contradicted, as he grabbed the feather out of Willy's hand.

"Relax, Jojo, we're just having fun with the sparrow. We're looking for our stash of food," Willy cajoled, looking very sly.

"Maybe you forgot where you hid it," Zeke proposed, his tone suggesting a newly acquired bravery, probably because Jojo was his friend.

"I'll get you, you little twerp," was Willy's angry response, further evidenced by his sticking out his neck and fluffing his feathers in an intimidating, aggressive posture.

"You'll do no such thing," Jojo yelled in admonishment. "You're in **my** oak tree now, and on **my** turf!"

"All right! I hear you." Willy balked. "But watch your back, sparrow," he threatened, quickly taking flight.

"You guys get going," Jojo told the sparrows. "I won't be able to control a mob of crazy crows."

"Okay, Jojo. Thanks for everything," Zeke expressed with gratitude. "Come on, Hawk, let's get breakfast," he called to his companion.

The invitation sounded great to Hawk, who was starving.

"Where are you going?" he asked.

"You'll see," Zeke answered briefly.

Zeke flew to a neighborhood of neatly lined houses with backyards, followed by Hawk. The community was located near the downtown area called Hummingbird Heights. The sun was out in full splendor by now. Zeke parked himself atop a wooden fence.

"Let's wait here," Zeke told Hawk.

"Wait here for what?" Hawk asked with great curiosity.

"Patience, my friend. You'll see," answered Zeke. Changing the subject, Zeke had a question of his own. "What's with the white feather, anyway?"

"It was my father's," Hawk informed Zeke.

"Where are you from, Hawk, and what do you want with Crow City?" Zeke asked additionally.

"I'm from Meadowlarksville," Hawk answered. "You sure do ask a lot of questions."

"Hey, chill out! What's with you, anyway?" Zeke declared. "Here I am trying to help you, and you jump on my case."

"Sorry," was Hawk's honest comeback, not wanting to say too much. He still wasn't trustful of many birds, nor of people.

"No big deal," Zeke assured the visiting sparrow.

"What happened to your eye?" Hawk questioned Zeke.

"Who's asking questions now?" Zeke challenged.

"Well, you don't have to tell me. No big deal, right?" Hawk mimicked.

Zeke started to say something, but was interrupted by a cardinal named Red, who had also perched himself on the fence.

"Oh no," Zeke said, disappointed. "I thought he was out of town."

Hawk noticed the fence was starting to fill up with different kinds of city birds. They were unlike other birds; more aggressive than he was used to.

"Who's the newcomer?" Red wanted to know.

"He's just visiting," Zeke replied reluctantly.

"Well, there are rules, Zeke, and you know it," stressed Red.

Great, Hawk thought. *More rules.*

"Yeah, I know the rules, Red. Just this one time give him a break," Zeke petitioned.

"Okay," Red agreed. "But he will have to get the seeds off the ground, and all the sunflower seeds are mine! There's no room at the bird feeder."

Suddenly, a woman came out of the back door of her house and emptied a bag of seed into the bird feeder. Zeke was looking at his watch.

Right on time, he thought.

Suddenly, what had been only a few birds multiplied into an extensive flock of aggressive city birds.

"You'll have to be quick, Hawk, or you'll be left with nothing but dirt, to eat," Zeke warned his fellow sparrow.

By now, Hawk was so hungry he could eat anything. But he knew he would be competing with very experienced and forceful birds.

"Come get your food, little birdies," the lady summoned. "But do watch out for the neighbor's cat; he relishes little birdies!"

"What? There's a cat I have to watch out for?" Hawk said in distress.

"How did you know that, Hawk?" Zeke asked, confused.

Hawk was about to answer but was cut off by a landing swarm of birds. Breakfast had just become a wild feeding frenzy.

"Oh, for the comforts of home," Hawk mused longingly. Having gotten a rather meager meal, Hawk was still hungry. Now he would have to learn to survive.

What he didn't know was how much he would have to learn and overcome, to survive in this rowdy city, even to the point of fleeing, to save his life.

Chapter Eleven
Singing for Food

It was nearly lunchtime and Hawk was still hungry. Zeke had brought up the idea of going downtown to Pigeon Square so Hawk could scrounge around for food. Pigeon Square was surrounded by many restaurants and shops.

"Okay, Hawk, I'll teach you how to be quicker than lightning," Zeke told his feathered visitor as they landed on an empty table on the square.

Quickly, Hawk began to understand how desperately he would need all the help he could get, in this town of ruffians. Many people were sitting at the tables, outside. Some were throwing food to the birds, even though a posted sign stating, "Do not feed the pigeons," prohibited it. A hoard of pigeons waited around for the scraps.

Suddenly a piece of bread went flying through the air, landing amid a crowd of pigeons. It was snatched up in seconds.

"Okay, okay, there will be more," Zeke explained.

"Wow, what pigs!" Hawk said firmly. He was not used to pigeons. They were rude and boisterous. "Hey, I've got it!" Hawk exclaimed in unbelief.

"Got what?" asked Zeke. "You've got nothing, my friend.

"No," Hawk enlightened Zeke. "I've got an idea! I will just sing one of my beautiful songs!" But in his heart, he wondered, *Has it come to this – singing for food?*

Hawk had always been shy when it came to singing, despite having been told many times that he had a beautiful voice. Singing for food, however, was indeed a different matter; a desperate one!

"What did you just say?" Zeke asked. "That's the funniest thing I've ever heard!" he went on. By now he was laughing so hard that he started coughing forcefully, nearly choking.

Hawk snapped back, "I don't think that's comical at all, Zeke! I'm really hungry!"

"Got it! That's cool," Zeke said calmly. "I'll just stand around and watch. This I've got to see!" he snickered.

Hawk fluttered to a table closer to where the people were eating. As he opened his mouth, out flowed a glorious tune. The melody surprised even him. It was a song he had learned at home, about a wonderful Creator who made all things beautiful. Immediately, he attracted the attention of all the pigeons who were still clamoring for food.

"What is that bird doing?" asked one very plump pigeon.

"Seems to me he's singing for his food," another explained.

"How absurd!" a third pigeon observed.

Hawk kept on singing.

A little girl, who was at the restaurant with her mother, listened with great interest to Hawk's singing. "Mama, let me feed the little bird some food. He sings so beautifully!" the child noticed.

"He certainly does," the mother said in agreement. "We'll get him something special."

"The little bird sings songs as I sing in Sunday school," the little girl mentioned as she started humming to the tune.

"Oh, Annie," her mother remarked, "I think you have quite an imagination – to sing along with the sparrow!"

In amazement, Zeke got over his laughter in a snap. He flew closer to Hawk, to hear him better.

"Come on, little bird, sing some more Sunday school songs!" the little girl prompted.

Hawk was singing so beautifully, other people started to notice. Some even started to sing softly or whistle along with him. Hawk sang with all of his heart, as he looked up at the sky. It seemed more blue than usual; the clouds brighter, appearing almost within reach.

As Hawk attentively beheld all this beauty, he was suddenly astonished at what he discovered. Perched on one of the clouds was the eagle, Malachi! Again, Hawk set his eyes on the creature's sparkling wings, powdered, it would seem, with gold dust. Behind him were at least several dozen angels, arrayed in white, all joining in with Hawk's magnificent songs. Hawk was so taken by the majestic display, he unconsciously repeated the same verse several times. He was relieved to see that hardly anyone noticed his mistake amidst all the singing, humming, and whistling they were doing, enjoying such a wonderful time!

Hawk focused on Malachi, who was now even more radiant with glory. He was nodding with pleasure at the spectacular sight. Malachi gave Hawk the 'thumbs up' sign, in approval. Hawk sang himself happy. He even forgot he was hungry, though he was well rewarded with tasty seeds and morsels of all sorts. Even the pigeons got a share of the food. Hawk was quite satisfied for the time being, forgetting all his troubles.

Hawk wondered if anyone besides himself had seen the heavenly manifestation. He was content that as people walked by, they were making comments such as, "My! Doesn't that little sparrow sing beautifully!"

One person even said, "He's awesome!"

Zeke chuckled to himself, then wondered how he would be able to profit from this talented singer. After all, Hawk needed him, in this quite uncivilized city; not to mention that Zeke was resourceful! While meditating on this, Zeke heard a 'caw-caw' sound in the sky, now darkening with the presence of many crows.

"Oh, oh; the party's over!" Zeke's exclamation was loud and edgy, as he lifted his eyes toward the crows.

Hawk's attention also turned to the crows. "Why, what's that..."

Hawk didn't get to finish his question because Zeke was nervously interrupting him. "They're coming to see what's up! When a flock of us gathers like this," Zeke pointed to those around him, "the crows always want to cause trouble."

Hawk looked in all directions. He had not realized how many birds had come to investigate what was going on. A couple of finches were talking amongst themselves, and a comment was heard from one of them, stating, "Well, I've never heard such delightful singing as this!"

"Neither have I," the other stated. "We'll have to find out who that was."

Hawk was about to speak to them when Zeke yelled out, "Let's go, Hawk! Unless you want trouble!"

"Where are we off to?" Hawk asked, with a certain fear.

"Anywhere but here!" hollered Zeke, frantically taking off.

Hawk and Zeke left Pigeon Square just in time. The hostile crows had landed in the square and were bullying the other birds. They were even bold enough to intimidate some of the people.

Chapter Twelve

A Very Bizarre Dream

Late afternoon that day, Zeke wanted to introduce Hawk to some of his connections downtown, who also happened to be his friends. Hawk thought it would be best to rest awhile in a nice shade tree before going, or even take a long nap. The eventful experiences of the day had been exhausting for him.

Zeke agreed they would find a place to rest for an hour or so. Hawk was not used to this fast-paced life.

"Where are we going?" Hawk asked with interest.

"Oh, it's a surprise," Zeke said.

Hawk cringed. He didn't like surprises. He wondered what Zeke was up to. Finally, they found an oak tree that was squeezed in between two buildings, off the main street. No sooner had Zeke and Hawk positioned themselves on a limb than they heard several sparrows calling out to Zeke.

"Hey, Zeke! Ole buddy, where have you been? Who's that with you?" the sparrows wanted to find out.

"This is Hawk, a famous singer, and I'm his agent," Zeke said boastfully.

"What?" Hawk cried out.

Zeke ignored him and went on. "He's on his way to fame, but is too modest to acknowledge it," he squawked excitedly.

"Oh, brother," Hawk said in disbelief.

"Tell us more!" the sparrows cried out.

The sparrows in Crow City were known for their singing, Hawk discovered. They were called the Crow City Song Sparrows. Richey, Lenny, Georgie, and Teddy. They were excited to hear about this "famous singer" visiting their town. The group was always competing with other sparrows and had formed a quartet among themselves. It was understandable that they wanted to hear all that Zeke had to say.

Hawk hopped over to another limb. He was just too tired to argue about his sudden "fame" and his so-called "agent." Hawk fell into a deep sleep that drowned out the voices of Zeke and his fellow sparrows.

As he dozed, Hawk dreamed he was back home with his mother, Mary and friend, Paxie. He and his friend were having fun and soon they decided to visit their private hideout. There, they splashed in the cool water, frolicking and laughing. Then Hawk saw faint images of his father, whom he had hardly known. His face appeared and faded as Hawk dreamed. The next image took Hawk into a thickly vegetated forest he had never seen before. It was breathtakingly lovely. There were all kinds of birds everywhere he looked, singing marvelous songs. There was a quartet that had exceptional talent.

As Hawk slumbered, Zeke's four musical friends were practicing nearby. Zeke was conducting the foursome.

In Hawk's dream, the rabbits ran through the forest, chasing one another. Squirrels and foxes played games and had great fun. Next, Hawk saw a nest with newborn baby birds calling out for their mother. A doe was strolling among the trees, her brown-eyed fawn skipping alongside. As Hawk admired the panorama, he started chirping with the other birds. This was a much different environment than Hawk had ever seen. He had never been in a forest. Even the fragrances were delightful!

His dream continued, and in it, Hawk was truly enjoying the pine scents, the wildflowers, the honey, and the smoke. The smoke?

Where can that odor be coming from? Hawk wondered. As he pondered this oddity, he thought he heard a faint sound of thunder in the distance. The sound increased in volume, but now became more like hooves and feet running, pounding the forest floor.

The animals surrounding Hawk, large and small, were motionless for a brief moment. The tension in the atmosphere immediately became a very genuine fear. Then, to Hawk's astonishment, the animals fled in unison. The smell of smoke was extremely strong now, and overpowering, as Hawk witnessed a massive exodus of animals, fleeing for their lives.

The fire was menacing, devouring everything in its path. Hawk remembered the baby birds, and without hesitation flew at full speed to their rescue. The smoke was thick and suffocating. Hawk struggled to breathe, coughing and choking. He could barely see and was losing his bearings.

In his plight, Hawk promptly turned his attention to the angry flames that were lapping up the forest. His breathing more restrained now, Hawk felt his chest hurting.

"Oh no!" Hawk cried out in panic. "I'll never find the way out!" Hawk's head was spinning and he started to feel faint. He thought he was going to die in this inferno.

Then he thought he saw something appear in the distance. He squeezed his eyes shut, then opened them again. There, in the dense haze of smoke, the enormous face of a roaring lion came forth. It was faint at first, due to the heavy cloud of smoke. Hawk sensed that something extremely unusual was occurring. Every time the lion opened his mouth to roar, the fire and smoke would dissipate, as if being sucked up by a gigantic vacuum. When the atmosphere finally cleared, Hawk saw the giant figure. He had six enormous wings that propelled him through the forest sky.

"What an incredible sight!" Hawk uttered in awe. Was the smoke getting the better of him, the bewildered sparrow wondered. At that moment, the deafening roar of the lion burst throughout the forest. Then a welcomed yet unexpected rain shower began, increasing in density until every single flame flickered out.

The lion had now flown closer to Hawk as if coming to greet him. Hawk's body trembled and his beak quivered with emotion. Soon the lion was within speaking distance.

"Hawk!" the lion called. "Remember your destiny from the Most High!"

Those words penetrated Hawk's body and mind. Hawk, being consumed with fear, blurted out, **''What is your name**!'

The enormous lion responded, "Paxie is not here **this time**...my name is Judah."

With this odd answer, Judah vanished into a fiery cloud. Next, Hawk heard a faint voice that sounded to him like Paxie's.

"It can't be!" Hawk said in disbelief. "Paxie must be lost in the forest!" Hawk couldn't remember Paxie being with him, though and the huge lion did say Paxie was not here.

"Hawk! Hawk! Wake up, Hawk." Zeke was calling him.

Hawk opened his eyes to the realization that he had been dreaming. Confused, he jumped up alarmed, loudly saying, "I have to go find Paxie!"

"Paxie? Who's Paxie? Zeke asked.

"He's my buddy from Meadowlarksville," Hawk responded. "I was dreaming about a forest fire and a huge lion with six wings," he added in explanation.

"What?" Zeke asked, making no sense of Hawk's words. "That's a very bizarre dream, Hawk!"

Chapter Thirteen
Problems, Problems!

"A lion that flies? And he told you what? To find your destiny? What in the world does he mean by that? Aren't you a sparrow?" Zeke bombarded Hawk with all kinds of questions, all the while trying to hold in his laughter.

"Yes, I am, Zeke, and so are you. But don't you ever wonder why you're here?" answered Hawk, probingly.

"Well," said Zeke, "it never really occurred to me why, but what about joining our singing group? Seems to me you have a talent for singing. You put on a great show downtown at Pigeon Square. We were practicing melodies for hours. Of course, I was conducting," Zeke stated, very sheepishly, "while you were sleeping.

"Hawk, you could be the lead song sparrow. Our group will be called 'Zeke and his Crow City Song Sparrows'," Zeke continued. "I've already booked you for some shows. How about it, Hawk?"

"What?" asked Hawk. "I've never been in show business, under the spotlight!" he said, aghast, while he thought, *The audacity of Zeke to do such a thing!* Hawk imagined himself performing before an enormous audience. The prospect of this paralyzed him with fear. "Oh no way, Zeke! Pigeon Square is one thing, but an international song bird chorus is quite another!" Hawk answered, agitatedly.

"No, Hawk, you see... you'll start in public areas like street corners, market places, and parks," Zeke explained, as convincingly as he could.

"I'm here in Crow City on business!" Hawk blurted out, annoyed with Zeke.

"What business?" Zeke asked. "You never did tell me why you were here. Besides that, I've noticed that you seem to understand what people are saying when they speak."

"Yes, I do," Hawk confirmed. "Although, there are some people I'd rather not understand," he said, contorting his face. Hawk stopped short of sharing his problem with Zeke concerning the two people who had taken his father's life.

"Oh, dear! Like who?" Zeke asked, anxious to know.

"Like those two who murdered my dad!" Hawk answered in an angry exclamation. Remembering the not-too-long-ago episode of darkness around him, he tried to be calm.

Zeke jumped back, unmistakably disturbed. "Oh no!" he gasped. "I didn't know there are some people out there that are mean!"

"Well, I was shocked myself!" answered Hawk, irately raising his voice.

After a few moments, Hawk calmed down again and said, "Well, my mother told me that there are some that are good." He then related to Zeke how the little girl and her mother had kindly buried his dad.

"Well, what are you going to do about that?" questioned Zeke.

"That's why I'm here in Crow City," said Hawk, "to find them."

"Oh, I thought you were here to find your destiny, which is singing with us, Hawk!" insisted Zeke. "Besides, what are you going to do when you find them?"

"I don't know," Hawk answered as if meditating on something. "Maybe I just want to ask them why they did it."

"Wow!" Zeke answered in astonishment. "You're going to talk to them? You've got problems, Hawk!" he answered in a heavy tone, then paused for an extended moment, finally continuing. "I'll make you a deal. If I help you find these two bad people, will you sing with us?"

"Well, let me think about that," responded Hawk, with uncertainty.

"Let's go get some food," Zeke said. "We'll go downtown to find another restaurant. Then you can practice singing."

"We don't have to go, Zeke," Hawk pointed out. "I have enough food here for both of us." While pulling out his supply of edibles he'd gotten at Pigeon Square, Hawk accidentally pulled out his dad's white feather.

"That's quite a feather," noted Zeke remembering he saw it earlier.

"This was my father's feather," was Hawk's quick response, as he immediately placed the feather back into his backpack. "This is all I have left to remember him by." This prompted Hawk to ask his feathered friend, "What about your father, Zeke?"

"My father was flying in a great thunderstorm, and got lost," Zeke reported. "That's what my mother told me," he added.

"Oh gosh!" Hawk said in surprise. "And where is your mother, Zeke?"

"Well, she spends her time looking for him. She doesn't stay in one place long enough for us to have a home," Zeke explained in dismay.

"What happened to your eye?" asked Hawk wanting to change the subject

Hesitating, and reluctant to speak about it, Zeke answered, "Well, let's put it this way, there are also some pretty bad birds out there."

Hawk decided to not press the issue any further.

"You know, Hawk, my mother even looks into windows to try to find my dad. She thinks he may have been captured and locked up in a cage!" Zeke said.

Both shuddered at the thought of such an act. Each of them had heard stories, as youngsters, of other birds that had been apprehended and kept incarcerated in bird cages. They also heard about birds accidentally flying into people's houses and never coming out again. Of course, they didn't know whether the latter was a true story or not.

"Let's look in the windows!" exclaimed Zeke. "Maybe we can find what we're looking for, in there."

"Good idea, Zeke. We'll start tomorrow," answered Hawk, realizing it was getting late.

"You're right. We need to find a place to sleep tonight," was Zeke's idea, as the sun started to set.

The two flew off to find shelter, well aware that this was not a safe place in which to be out at dark.

Unbeknownst to them, trouble was already brewing in Crow City.

Chapter Fourteen

The Angelic Choir

awk woke up early the next morning, in the place Zeke found for them to sleep the night before: on the window ledge of a worn-down church building. Arising to the sound of beautiful music, Hawk wondered whose angelic voices he could be hearing, since Zeke was still asleep. He eagerly peeked inside the windows. Though sleepy yet curious, he wanted to investigate these enchanting voices. Hawk thought it was quite early for anyone, even birds, to be singing. As he peered, he suddenly exclaimed, "Oh my!" expressing what his eyes could hardly believe.

Rubbing his eyes, he focused on a huge golden stairway that started at the floor of the church and shot through its roof. The strange situation though it was, the structure didn't seem to damage the building in the slightest. It looked as if it was part of the building and the stairs had been there the whole time.

Then Hawk saw angels going up and down the golden staircase, carrying all sorts of musical instruments, so shiny they nearly blinded him. Squinting to get a sharper look, Hawk saw the huge heavenly beings bringing harps, drums, flutes, and even a large piano. They were all quite busy accomplishing their assignments.

In one corner of the room, twenty angels were singing in choir form. They seemed to be having a great time. Next, deep laughter resounded throughout the large room, while an angel who had been bowed over, hands on his knees, then began slapping his thigh, chortling, "Oh those humans, they truly are amusing!"

Meanwhile, the angels on the golden stairs were busy conversing. Hawk heard one of them say, "Let's hurry, Jacob. The people will be coming soon, and it'd be nice if all the musical instruments would be ready." Continuing his conversation, the first angel named Joel, fervently yet authoritatively stated, "The Master said it was time to get them out of the storehouse."

"Yes, the storehouse of blessings!" Jacob responded smiling and added, "We could be very busy bringing blessings down to Earth if people only believed the Master wants to bless them!"

I wonder who the 'Master' is, Hawk thought.

The music played on as Zeke slept. Hawk was so taken by the beautiful melodic sounds that he wanted to join in himself. But in a flash, the heavenly beings one by one started to disappear. Even the stairway vanished.

"Oh!" thought Hawk, "I wonder where they went!" All at once, he heard footsteps on the pathway outside that led to the church door.

It was Frank, the janitor who had been volunteering at the church for some time. He'd always been the first one to open the church doors as part of his Sunday routine. This morning he seemed a little bored, and yawning, he mumbled to himself, "Here we go again. I wonder what today will bring." Noticing some bright rays of light appearing to be shooting out of the church windows, he was puzzled as to who could've left the lights on.

Jiggling his keys, Frank opened the door and was instantly blasted by lights so bright and dazzling he thought he would pass out. Leaning forward to steady himself, he plopped onto one of the chairs, dropping his keys as he fell.

Amazed, Frank stared squinty-eyed at the luminous musical instruments that radiated brilliant rays. "I must be dreaming or I've gone to heaven," he muttered to himself. "But I don't remember dying!"

The next moment he noticed an angel walking toward him. His instinct was to run, but he couldn't move his feet, even as the heavenly being drew near. Frank paled and started to tremble, as the angel smiled and looked right at him, then vanished. Frank fell forward from his chair onto his hands and knees in astonishment.

"No one will believe this!" he assuredly exclaimed to himself, quite unconvinced as to whether he was dreaming or whether he had died. Pondering upon this, Frank picked himself from the floor and collected his keys, hands still shaking. He heard footsteps now, and familiar voices outside. He tried to yell out, only to discover he was speechless. Frank listened as the following conversation ensued:

"This is the pastor's last day here," said an elderly lady named Alice, as she approached the walkway. She took a handkerchief out and blew her nose. Tears streamed down her cheeks.

"Yes," responded her friend, named Della. "He's been so downhearted since his wife passed, and now he has two little ones to raise without a mom..." Della paused briefly, then added, "I declare, aren't the Lord's way mysterious?"

Alice cried all the more.

"Now now, dear Alice," Della prompted. "You've been so faithful to cook for him and his family."

Still sobbing, Alice spoke softly, "Thank you, Della, but you also helped greatly, doing the wash and cleaning his house."

Hawk, who was still observing, was almost brought to tears himself.

Alice went on, "The youngest boy, Tommy, said he saw two angels taking his mommy up to heaven."

This time it was Della who burst into tears, as she declared, "Tommy, who's only four, believes such sweet things…"

Unexpectedly, Alice interrupted announcing, "Look, bright lights are coming out of the church!"

"Well, why in heaven's name did Frank turn on every light in the church?" Della asked.

Before Alice could answer, more voices were heard coming up the walkway, from church members who wondered the same thing.

Zeke was fully awake now, with all the bright lights and voices around him. He asked Hawk, "What's with all these blinding lights Hawk? I need sunglasses! And were you practicing your music? I heard some beautiful music. I like these fellows from heaven you're always talking about!"

"Oh!" Hawk replied. "These huge feathered fellows from heaven, called angels, were bringing all kinds of musical instruments to earth on a golden stairway! They said that apparently, the people have been 'praying' for them, whatever that means."

Zeke looked kind of funny at Hawk and asked, "Oh Hawk, have you been dreaming again?"

"No," Hawk answered, still wondering what "praying" could mean.

Chapter Fifteen

The Miracle of the Musical Instruments

$\int$ everal of the church's choir members were the first to abruptly rush through the doors, knocking Frank onto his hands and knees again, jarring his keys loose a second time. One choir member was so mesmerized with the musical instruments, which now seemed to have lost some of their brilliance, he tripped over Frank and landed on his hands and knees himself. Numerous choir members were utterly speechless as they stared in awe. Others continued to mill in steadily, including Alice and Della.

The tumultuous sounds of "Oohs" and "Aahs" could be heard from the approaching members.

Overcome with joy, Alice burst out, "Why, it's a **miracle**!"

"Yes, this is a miracle indeed!" declared a rapturously overwhelmed Della.

"We have been praying for these instruments for a whole year!" exclaimed Minnie, one of the staff members, as she excitedly jumped up and down. Clamoring, she added, "Why these instruments are so brilliant, they seem to have lights in them!"

Minnie's son, Billy, responded quickly in a shout, "That's 'cause they just came from heaven, Mommy!"

The boy immediately joined the other kids, as they ran together to behold the unbelievable sight. The adults followed joyfully, many still rubbing their eyes in disbelief and squinting to avoid the glare. Some were staring up into the ceiling.

Still in amazement, Alice glanced at a beautiful mahogany guitar, trimmed in gold, as she drew closer for a better look. On it was inscribed, "Janie Cox," the name of the pastor's wife. The instrument looked as if Janie had always been playing it! Yet, it had broken a year ago.

"My word," stated Alice excitedly, "this even has her name on it!" Alice then grabbed Della by the hand to show her, while stating in a solemn tone, "Look, her name is even on it! My heavens, she's been gone exactly one year ago today! How utterly mysterious the Lord's ways can be!"

Having been attentively watching this strange activity, Hawk was more than overwhelmed by it all. In an audible voice, he questioned, "I wonder where heaven is?"

As he munched on a seed cake, Zeke's response was, "I don't know, but isn't that where your angels are?

"Let's play these instruments and worship," said David, one of the lead singers, as he helped Frank to his feet.

"What a wonderful idea," stated Jack, who customarily played piano during worship. Lately, he had not done so, because it was out of service. Now, here was a brand new piano before them. Jack walked toward it, moving carefully among the crowded room full of congregation members, fully aware that he had just tripped over Frank.

The musicians and singers assumed their regular positions. This was such a grand event, what with every instrumentalist playing a brand new heavenly instrument. The song they selected was *Amazing Grace*, and the singers were pleasantly surprised to each have gotten a "new voice."

Hawk loved this particular song, and he so wanted to sing along with them. He noticed there were song sparrows on the other ledges, and some were already singing along. So he joined in, as Zeke listened.

At that moment, the pastor walked in with his two children. He had immediately noticed, of course, all the brand new instruments that still sparkled brightly, although his eyes did not seem overcome by the glimmer. He had wanted to ask where the instruments had come from. Instead, when he opened his mouth, he broke out in song, astounded at his newfound singing ability. All the children could do was to stare intently at Dad and the instruments.

Precipitously, four-year-old Tommy expressed in delight, "Look, Daddy, the angels!"

The angels had returned, and this time, Malachi was with them. Malachi appeared more radiant than ever. A luminous glory surrounded him. The faces of the congregation glowed, the children's faces were radiant, as they all praised joyfully in song.

Looking upward, above the choir members' heads, and seeing the glorious angels for the first time, Della ecstatically exclaimed, "Oh, I *'see'* now what the children *'see'*!"

"I see them too," whispered Alice, who seemed to have lost her voice.

After the song was over, Frank had a desire to pick up the gold-trimmed guitar that had the name "Janie Cox" engraved on it. Taking it, he instantly handed it to the pastor. At that gesture, the eyes of almost everyone in the room welled up with tears. Even Zeke, who was peering in, became sentimental. The pastor played a wonderful song about "The Lamb."

Hawk noticed in silent surprise that the angels were all solemnly kneeling. Malachi had also joined the angels in all his splendor and glory. He also noticed that the lion with the six huge wings, the one that had been in his dream in the forest, had joined them. As he sang,

Hawk noticed the lion was watching him with admiration. Hawk looked at the other song sparrows perched outside the window and noticed the lion seemed pleased with them as well.

When the service was over, Hawk made a beeline to join the other sparrows. He listened as numerous joyful church members talked about "the miracle," and how elated they were that the pastor was not leaving after all. Many people continued to sing, dance, and laugh with great joy. Even Frank felt as if he had a new lease on life – one without boredom, to be sure.

Hawk introduced himself to the sparrows who were singing on the other window ledges. Zeke, undoubtedly, was not going to miss out on this gathering.

"I love the way you guys sing," proclaimed Hawk.

"We delight in singing with these church members," indicated Rex, one of the sparrows.

There were at least four of them. Hawk could sense peace as he remained among them. He was deeply touched by their passion and warmth. It seemed these sparrows had truly found their destiny; something he, himself, was supposed to be looking for. Unbeknownst to him, however, this quest would appear to elude him as he continued to his next destination.

Rex asked Hawk if he'd like to join their singing group. Zeke emerged just then and announced, "Hello, my name is Zeke, and I'm Hawk's singing agent!"

"Oh," said Rex, "you sing in a group?"

Hawk was about to answer when Zeke swiftly interrupted, "Yes, it's called 'Crow City Song Sparrows,'" and turning toward Hawk, he announced, "Hawk will be performing at Canary Row today at 5:00 p.m."

Hawk's mouth dropped with astonishment at this unexpected outcome.

Up to this point, Hawk had had quite a peaceful day. Now he wondered whether he was ready for whatever was ahead. He recalled that the only singing he had done was at Pigeon Square. Hawk was not at all certain this was part of his destiny.

Chapter Sixteen

Canary Row

After their good-byes to Hawk's new friend, Rex, and the other sparrows, Zeke and Hawk flew to Canary Row on the oceanfront. There was still much excitement at the church, and Hawk felt disappointed at having to depart so suddenly. Zeke, on the other hand, was enthused about Hawk's debut at Canary Row. He had big plans for the Crow City Song Group, which included Hawk and four other song sparrows, Lenny, Teddy Georgie, and Richey. Zeke and Hawk had agreed to meet the singers for lunch at Canary Row Bakery and then have their rehearsal afterward.

He had met the group a day earlier after he'd fallen asleep on a downtown window ledge. It was on that occasion that Hawk had experienced a horrible nightmare in which he'd been trapped in a forest fire. Boy, was that a bizarre dream! But then, hadn't he also seen an enormous six-winged lion this very morning?

Hawk was quite animated about going to Canary Row, a quaint town filled with activity and commotion, and a vast array of tantalizing smells. Besides, he'd never been to the ocean before in his life — what an adventure!

Restaurants and shops of all varieties lined up along the beautiful beachfront. This was a gathering place for canaries who had accidentally escaped from their owners; some had even escaped from pet stores. Word had it that Crow City was a haven for canaries since they not only loved to sing, but they truly enjoyed being entertained. There certainly was a lot of "entertainment" at Canary Row. The town had rapidly grown from a few canaries to hundreds, as more and more made this their homestead. It was the crows that had given Canary Row its name, since they were in charge of entertainment.

The intense aroma of fish and fresh-baked bread permeated the air. Pleasant scents from the many flower species growing near the beach filled the air. Bright colors of red, yellow, and purple decorated the environment, attracting hummingbirds galore. The boisterous seagulls filled the air with exhilarating squawking sounds, one to another. All the while, the seals joined the clamor with their loud "barking" and begging for food. Additionally, people yelling to their children unmindfully contributed to the noise making, competing, as it were, with the ocean waves as they collided against the sand and rocks.

"What are those?" asked Hawk, focusing on the squawking flying creatures above him.

"Oh, those are scavengers," explained Zeke nonchalantly, as he pointed to the seagulls. Hawk had never seen such beings. "They won't bother us," continued Zeke, "they're just riotous and fight with each other." As Zeke emphasized his point, two seagulls wrangled over a poor dead fish they'd found on the beach.

This type of competitive display seemed repulsive to Hawk. He still stared in disbelief, aghast at the gross quarreling over a fish.

Abruptly, one of the seagulls came to a halt and yelled, "Mind your own business! This is ours!"

The shrieking seagull lost his hold on the fish just then, allowing his opponent to run off with the prize, leaving the embarrassed rival to chase frantically after him. Bewildered, Hawk wondered what on earth was Zeke getting him into, after watching such loathsome drama.

The two friends, Hawk and Zeke, arrived at the Canary Row Bakery just in time for lunch. All too soon, they heard, "Hey, Zeke ole buddy!" One of the quartet's song sparrows beckoned.

"Hey, Lenny! You know Hawk, here!" prompted Zeke as he landed in front of the bakery. The tempting savor of fresh bread made Hawk's mouth water. With all the turmoil, he'd taken no time to eat, and until now, hadn't realized how hungry he was.

Zeke and Hawk greeted the rest of the quartet – Lenny, Georgie, Richey, and Teddy. They were feasting now on crusty bread that people had tossed at them. Hawk gulped down some bread crumbs as quickly as he could, oblivious of the other singing group members staring at him. Even as he devoured the bread, the onlookers seemed to show a kind of admiration for Hawk. At that awkward moment, Hawk was suddenly aware that the singing birds were all attired in suits and ties. Food still in mouth, he blurted out, "Where do I get one of those?"

"One of what?" asked Zeke, as his huge beak examined a huge pastry crumb he'd found. He added as an afterthought, "You can have this one!"

"No, I mean, look at what they're wearing!" Hawk pointed out, almost in a panic.

Instantaneously Teddy, one of the four singers called out, "Not to worry, my friend. I have one for you!"

"Zeke told us you didn't have anything, except a big white feather! Is it magical or something?" asked Richey, another singer from the group.

"Okay, guys!" interrupted Zeke, "we need to rehearse. Hawk, go put on your suit."

Modest as he was, Hawk hid nearby to put on his suit. As he was dressing, he heard Zeke and the others talking about how famous they were going to be.

"Why we'll be known throughout Crow City!" remarked Lenny.

"...throughout the world!" Teddy exclaimed with great exuberance.

"Yes, I do believe the crows will be mighty pleased!" Zeke interjected confidently.

No doubt, the crows did love entertainment. They put on their shows among themselves at Crow Municipal Park, though they really couldn't sing. All they did was squawk and caw. This sparrow concert, on the other hand, would mean greater fame and patronage for Zeke and the crows. After all, the crows were the ones that ran the Crow City operations.

Chapter Seventeen

Show Biz

*C*anary Row was getting crowded with people and multiple kinds of birds. The canaries had circulated the word amongst themselves and other feathered friends that there was going to be a "Spectacular Show" tonight, to be presented by certain song sparrows.

Even now there was a large gathering of doves and finches, a few parrots, and of course, the crows. Even a few seagulls had come to witness "the show." Some birds were there only to see what the excitement was all about. The atmosphere at Canary Row was filled with singing, laughter, and excited anticipation. The canaries' love of singing became evident early on, as some of them trilled to the lyrics to "Old MacDonald," a tune learned from the people who'd been their previous owners.

"Hey, you're out of tune, Mickey!" expressed one radiantly yellow canary nicknamed Sunny.

"No! You're out of tune!" was the response made by Mickey himself.

"Uh, oh! What if I get out of tune?" remarked Hawk to himself. "Why I'll be the laughingstock of the town!" he surmised. A wave of panic overcame him. His thoughts were suddenly interrupted by a familiar voice.

"Hey Hawk!" was the call.

Turning to look, Hawk was surprised. It was the two sparrows he met that morning.

"What are you guys doing here?" inquired Hawk, then quickly interjected, "Boy! Am I glad to see you!"

"We came to hear you sing!" Rex answered with glee.

"And to give you a thumbs up!" the other sparrow stated, as Hawk glanced over at him. "Oh, you can call me Caleb," announced the second sparrow, demonstrating the "thumbs up" sign to Hawk.

"Well, I sure do need it!" replied Hawk, feeling the confidence their support gave him. "This suit is choking me!" clamored Hawk, pulling at his collar. "I must look like a stuffed cat!"

In a high-sounding voice, Zeke demanded, "Okay, places everyone!"

Never having heard Zeke talk at such a high pitch, Hawk could only stare at him in wonder. It seemed apparent to Hawk that he wasn't the only one who was apprehensive this evening.

The makeshift stage constructed of wooden crates was covered with yellow butterflies and flowers that the canaries had painted. How they loved the color yellow. And they wanted to make the show a success, even as they secretly hoped their contribution might get them in the crows' "good graces."

Again, the call was made as Zeke raised his voice over the loud chatter. "Places everyone!" He too was all dressed up in his suit and tie, looking smart and elegant. He even had a new patch over his eye. Zeke felt important in his leading role as choirmaster. They all looked so dapper, each one with a yellow carnation on his lapel.

Although the sun was setting at Canary Row, a vast supply of light illuminated the entire town. With the help of two seagulls, Zeke had managed to get the stage ready, with a neon sign that flashed, above the makeshift stage: "**Karaoke Tonight!**"

Unfamiliar with the term, Hawk asked himself, "I wonder what 'Karaoke" is?" Giddy with joy, he hopped onto the stage, taking his place in front of the quartet.

"I think it means, food," warbled Lenny, as he fidgeted with his tie. Lenny was always hungry.

"Don't talk about food right now," scolded Georgie. "I'm feeling stuffed in this suit. It's too tight on me, and I feel like —"

"Don't you dare say it, Georgie!" snapped Teddy. "You were warned not to wolf down all that food before the performance."

None of the quartet members had ever been to Canary Row before. There was just so much food and entertainment here that it was easy to overindulge. Teddy, however, was having such a grand time singing, dancing, and hopping about, his feet ached terribly. Now that he had to stand, he was standing on one foot, then the other.

By nightfall, the gathering of people, as well as varying kinds of birds, had grown quite extensive at Canary Row. Everyone together was creating a competitive mixture of sounds, noises, laughter, and singing. This was one of the few times and places in which the birds could safely be out at night and not have to be concerned about the presence of enemies. It seemed even the *predators* were "friendly."

Once more Zeke's voice resounded above the clatter. "My fellow birds and feathered friends, may I have your attention?" He seemed to have gotten his normal voice back. Turning toward a group of crows at the back seats, Zeke continued, "It's nice to see you all here, tonight!"

With the help of some eager seagulls who came to hear the singing group, the canaries had placed wooden crates to be used as seats. Hawk saw that these seagulls were polite and helpful, unlike the ones he had seen on the beach.

"I see that JoJo made it here, tonight! And, oh, there's Red. Welcome, Red, welcome! You won't be disappointed!" Zeke stated with heightened confidence.

It was still necessary that Zeke continued to yell above the chatter, as he requested, "Quiet, please!"

Suddenly JoJo stood up and fluffed his feathers, exclaiming, "Okay! Enough! Quiet! That got every feathered creature's attention. Even some people jumped.

Zeke continued in great joy, "It is my pleasure to introduce to you, the Crow City Song Sparrows, the finest singers in all of Crow City!"

A grand round of applause was heard next, coupled with clapping, shouting, and deafening whistling sounds. After this, Zeke's loud expression broke through, above the jubilant, boisterous crowd. "Also, my dear feathered friends, the music conductor for this evening is none other than **myself**, Zechariah Birdfield!"

Chapter Eighteen
Stage Fright

The rowdy applause had simmered down to a meager clap or two from the seagulls. But that quickly ended when the crows gave the seagulls a menacing stare. Then, the brightly flashing neon sign, "**Karaoke Tonight**," that hung over Hawk and the quartet, suddenly stopped, leaving the lights on continuously.

Trying to look important, Zeke took a bow and unexpectedly twirled rapidly around to face the song group, only to stumble and nearly drop his baton. Giggles and chuckles erupted throughout the entire crowd.

Hawk looked out at the extensive bird community, many of whom he didn't know. Of course, some he did, like Jojo and Red. Seeing them, however, brought little or no consolation to the timid little sparrow from a faraway place called Meadowlarksville.

Panic-stricken and confounded as he was, Hawk, surprisingly, was able to hear Zeke's voice clearly; not once, but twice. Zeke nodded to him now, to commence. Dry-mouthed and heart racing, Hawk opened his beak, only to hear a tiny squeak. Everyone's eyes were fixed on him with anticipation. Paralyzed with fear, Hawk felt dizzy, thinking he would surely faint. But when his eyes unexpectedly gazed upon Rex and Caleb in the crowd, he instantly recuperated, releasing a sigh of relief.

There was total silence in the crowd — so much so, one could've heard a feather drop. Nonetheless, Hawk didn't hear a feather drop: he saw one fall. Looking up to see where it came from, Hawk discovered a huge white feather floating above the crowd. It looked like his father's, except that it was much larger. He also saw small white feathers plummeting down on the crowd, much like he had seen at his father's gravesite.

Oddly enough, no one seemed to notice what was happening, except himself. Neither was anyone aware of the huge warrior angel that was present; the one Hawk had first seen in the 'hideout". The warrior angel communicated with him at that moment – not in audible words, yet what was transmitted was sure and author- itative, saying, *"Hawk, He shall cover you with His feathers, and under His wings, you shall take refuge."*

Hawk had not understood what the angel meant, but a peace came over him right at that instant – at the most appropriate time.

Abruptly, Hawk noticed that Zeke was tapping his baton loudly on his music stand, getting somewhat irritated. Just now, Hawk's unique talent was once again unleashed on the audience as he opened his beak and sang.

Many people attending the karaoke decided to sit outside and listen to the birds singing.

"Let's just sit outside tonight, Deb. It's so nice here, and the birds are singing so beautifully," Janie stated.

"Yes, let's do that," said Deb. "Funny though, I thought it might be way past their bed-time by now."

"Me too," said Janie.

"Well, this is Canary Row. So much goes on here," Deb added.

"Have you noticed how many birds are gathered here tonight? It's as if they had some sort of bird convention going on," stated Janie.

"Yeah, like some bird concert," noted Deb.

Hawk's singing was captivating. By this time, great numbers of people were seated outdoors. Some even picked up a tune and started whistling and singing, as they meandered by the "bird concert." At this point, many birds from far-away cities had arrived to hear Hawk and the quartet singing. Word had spread everywhere about how exquisite Hawk's singing voice was. Some birds even came from as far away as Meadowlarksville. Hawk himself had become so focused on his performance, he didn't recognize one particular face in the crowd, from that city.

Chapter Nineteen
A Familiar Face

Fully determined to find his buddy, Paxie flew into Crow City leaving behind him everything and everyone in Meadowlarksville. Before Paxie left on his mission to find Hawk, he had a visit with Mary and Jake. It seemed that life was no longer the same without his "best buddy."

"Oh, how I wish Hawk was here. I sure do miss him!" groaned Paxie. "I hope Hawk's mom knows where I can find him." Tears were flowing from his eyes once again as he neared Hawk's home.

Mary shared with Paxie about her last day with Hawk, and how hard it had been for him to hear the sad news about his father's untimely death. The shocking news had affected him so deeply that he vowed to get even with the two big bullies who had dealt his dad this dastardly deed. Mary continued, "I know Hawk will surely go to Hootersville and visit his father's gravesite." Tears streaming from her eyes, she noted to Paxie in a softer, hardly audible tone, "I don't know where he will go," she exclaimed with her beak quivering.

Attentive to what was being said, Jake abruptly interrupted the conversation, saying, "Maybe he went to Crow City!"

Mary gasped at the mention of the town. **"Crow City!** Why that place is full of ruffians and seedy birds that hang out everywhere!" She spoke with alarm.

Instantly, Jake realized he said the *wrong thing*. He quickly added, "Then again, maybe he hadn't!"

Paxie was all ears, listening to Mary and Jake as they continued conversing about whether Hawk had gone to Crow City or not. Inadvertently, Jake had opened a can of worms that Mary just couldn't swallow. Yet, Paxie was truly worried that his dear friend Hawk would encounter danger and never see him again. He would leave immediately in the morning, a time he knew his parents would be gone. Of course, he would leave a letter.

In the town of Hootersville, Paxie stopped at Hawk's father's gravesite to find clues from his friend. Mary had drawn him a map, showing the location of the rosebush, Paxie found the gravesite, but no clues where Hawk could be. With no further delay Paxie flew off to Crow City.

Crow City looked big and frightening to Paxie upon his arrival. For one thing, the city birds flew entirely too fast for his liking, nearly knocking him right out of the sky.

"Hey, you!" shouted an angry crow at Paxie, "Out of the way. This is the fast lane."

"Oh, no!" Paxie exclaimed. "The last thing I want is to tangle with those crows again."

Thinking it would be best to rest awhile, Paxie landed on a gigantic sign. Unbeknownst to him, pictured on that very sign were the Crow City Song Sparrows, featuring Zeke and Hawk as evening performers at Canary Row. Paxie was quite disheveled and dying of hunger after harrowingly escaping a gang of loudly threatening, malevolent crows at Crow City municipal Park. He'd had to give up his food supply to a crow named Willy, as other crows chased Paxie out of the area. From then on, Paxie learned to hide amidst the crowds; an escape technique to avoid the villains.

Enjoying his short respite on the sign and catching his breath, Paxie began to wonder concerning Hawk's whereabouts.

"This is a city to be feared!" he thought out loud as he reflected on Hawk. Filled with emotion, Paxie began to weep with sadness, still unaware of the singing sparrows' image on the sign.

Then, as a couple of doves joined him atop the sign, one of them commented, "Look, Harriet, these are the singers I was talking about. The lead singer's name is Hawk It's their debut! Word had spread quickly throughout Crow City amongst the feathered crowd. Zeke being their manager and publicity agent set things in motion. Zeke had connections with the crows who arranged the large sign. " Let's go see, Harold. Maybe we can get us some front row seats!" And off they flew, leaving Paxie dumbfounded.

After cautiously asking for directions from some feathered strangers, Paxie arrived at the makeshift stage the birds had built in Canary Row. He still could hardly believe that his friend, Hawk, would be performing in front of a crowd.

"This could not be the Hawk I know!" he expressed, astounded. "It just has to be another sparrow named Hawk. After all, he did look different on the sign."

"Exquisite!" squawked Winnie, a female seagull seated in the deluxe seats, along with some upper-class seagulls.

"Marvelous, marvelous!" yelled out a huge male seagull called Norman, clapping boisterously, while Hawk sang his beautiful, captivating songs

Hawk warbled fun songs, happy songs, sad and rhyming songs. But one song was so melancholic it gripped the hearts of all. Sniffling resounded all around; teary faces everywhere. One canary wailed so loudly, he had to be escorted out. Even people walking by were weepy. A young man named Mark joined the lament of others; and a girl named, Lisa, uttered, barely audibly, "I've never been moved to such sadness by a song!"

It turned out that Hawk was singing about a fellow sparrow whose life had been cut short by two bullies, leaving behind a wife and son. Hawk had to pause to weep, which brought on more weeping from the audience. Another canary had to be escorted out due to his anguished sobbing.

The weary Paxie, who was among the crowd, suddenly jolted to a halt as he realized, "Why that's Hawk up there, and he's singing about his dad. I must get to him." Paxie reacted quickly.

The singing quartet and Hawk were nearly finished with their performance now. But Zeke, sitting on the ground, wept so profusely, he dropped his baton. Continuing his song, Hawk looked around the crowd, hoping to find Zeke. He gazed for a second at a face he thought familiar, mentally inquiring to himself, *Could that be Paxie?* Hawk had trouble recognizing his friend because he remembered Paxie as always looking tidy, never a feather out of place. This fellow, on the other hand, was very dirty, with tattered clothes.

Shifting his focus to Zeke, who was now picking himself up off the ground, Hawk ended his song with great passion that left the audience in ecstatic joy. Zeke then took his place for the final act.

Tears wiped away now, he beamed with composure, as he announced, "My fine feathered friends, let's give another grand round of applause to Hawk and the Crow City Song Sparrows for an outstanding performance."

An enormous uproar of clapping and yelling ensued.

What took place next was most unexpected and astonishing. The clamorous crowd launched forward with great force, attempting to flock around Zeke and the singing group. Paxie was trampled amidst the crowd. Two crows serving as security guards struggled to hold back the advancing feathered pack. In hopes of restoring some semblance of order, they fiendishly shoved the overly excited fans back, to allow Zeke, Hawk, and the quartet to escape from the makeshift stage. Seats and debris were tossed everywhere as great chaos prevailed all around.

It was almost midnight by the time Zeke, Hawk, and the rest of the quartet were able to find a safe place to rest and call it a night.

Chapter Twenty
Sarah

Jolted out of a deep sleep, Hawk awakened to a pounding sound against the windows on the ledge where he and the other feathered performers were sleeping. Too excited to fall asleep, after the bird concert, he heard the song group talking and singing 'til the wee hours of the morning. Again, Hawk heard a knock on the windows, only this time it was much louder; a sound that woke up Zeke, who sleepily yelled out, "Come in!" Then, just as suddenly, he was back asleep again and snoring.

"Someone please answer the door!" mumbled Georgie, sleepy-toned.

"Or the window," Hawk added, as he looked up to see a pale little face staring at him with a puzzled look. Fully awake by now, Hawk stared straight back at the peeking face, thinking out loud, "I wonder if this is an angel?"

Zeke heard and mumbled in response, "Oh no-o-o-o. Here we go-o-o-o. Angels again?"

Ignoring Zeke's comment, Hawk mused, "She seems a bit small." Suddenly, his thoughts were interrupted as the window opened, banging against the wall and startling Hawk, while waking the others.

"Are you an angel?' Hawk inquired, realizing that he was stuttering as he spoke.

With a little giggle, Sarah replied, "No, but I have seen them; two of them, to be exact." "My name is Sarah," she continued, "and I have **never** seen a bird in a suit and tie before."

Hawk looked down at his wrinkled suit. "Oh no," he blurted out in embarrassment, smoothing out the wrinkles and straightening his tie.

"You're a song sparrow," she exclaimed. "I love the way you sing." Suddenly noticing that the sparrow could not only sing but speak also, she pointed out, "And you speak, too."

"Yes, and my name is Hawk."

Trying to put on an air of importance, despite his disheveled appearance, Hawk declared, deep voice and all, "Well, I've been able to talk since I was —"

Sarah didn't let him finish his statement as she interrupted with delight, "I want to hear you sing."

Fidgeting with his tie, Hawk nervously responded, "Well, uh, I... I don't know..."

Sarah interrupted one more time, pleading, "Please, Hawk; please sing me a song? I never get to hear music in this lonely room."

The warmth and melancholic sound in Sarah's voice deeply touched Hawk's feelings. He could recall other times when he had noticed the same behavior from people while he sang. There were many questions Hawk wanted to ask Sarah at this point, such as, "Why are you in this lonely room, Sarah?" But as he looked at her in her silence, eyes saddened and filled with tears, he was very keenly aware of her sorrowful emotions. Quite clearly now, Hawk remembered seeing that kind of expression in other people and knew what that meant, so he spoke urgently, "Please, don't cry. I'll sing whatever you like."

Putting his thoughts aside then, Hawk began to sing his lamentation about his dad. As she listened to the melody, Sarah cried. Oddly, Zeke and the quartet began to whimper also, even as they slept.

Meanwhile, numerous kinds of birds were flying nearby, doing their errands. Stopping at the window, they joined the chorus of pitiful cries. Such pronounced wailing and sobbing caught the attention of a group of crows that were on patrol in the vicinity. Just as Hawk came to the end of his song, the Crow City Patrol landed on the window ledge, crowding out the sparrows and doves that had joined the bellowing bunch.

"What is going on here?" asked one of the crows, with his voice breaking up and taking a kerchief out of his vest. He tried to hold back the tears.

One of his comrades pushed against his shoulder, saying, "Oh Stanley, you old softy." Then he stated even more loudly, "Hey, *fellas,* look. Stanley's crying again."

Immediately an uproar of laughter began and mockery from the other comrades. Hysteria broke out; giggling and cackles; a few guffaws; the fun-poking comments against poor Stanley would not let up.

Aside from that, some of the crows were trying to do their duty by clearing the flock of birds off the ledge, even as they tripped over several crows who were actually on their backs on the ledge, laughing hysterically.

Sarah wiped her eyes as she watched in astonishment the enormous population of birds that had gathered outside her window. She was even more confounded by the group of aggressive crows that were antagonistically shoving other flocks of birds around.

By now, Zeke and the quartet were wide awake. What with all the commotion and tumultuous assembly, sleep was out of the question. Suddenly a shrilly loud whistle pierced the chaotic atmosphere.

Willy blew his whistle again, announcing, "Order! Order! Illegal assembly, here. Who is in charge of this group?" Looking around for answers, Willy saw Zeke and stated sarcastically, "Why it's Zechariah Birdfield.

Don't you know you can't have concerts without a permit?"

"Well, Willy, this isn't an official concert," explained Zeke. "Hawk was simply singing for that little angel over there, uh, I mean, that person," Zeke corrected himself, as he pointed to Sarah. He continued, "And of course, his marvelous singing attracted these fine and law-abiding citizens of Crow City."

"Well," squawked Willy, "I suppose we won't give you a fine this time; but just remember," he added in a shrewdly authoritative voice, "Crow City's new Ordinance 4625B states, 'No singing performances without a permit.' And incidentally, I'm the new Crow City Chair since Jojo retired last week."

Carefully clearing his throat, in an effort not to sound disappointed, Zeke's comeback was, "Oh, well now, Willy, *congratulations.*"

Zeke was disappointed. He had not only developed a business relationship with JoJo but also a friendly one. This whole time, Willy was observing Zeke's uneasiness, relishing the opportunity of exhibiting his newly inherited authority over Crow City's feathered citizens.

"Now Zeke," blurted out Willy, rudely interrupting his thoughts. "I want to talk to you about Hawk's next performance. I think you and I have an understanding, if you know what I mean." Willy tinkered with his patrol badge, all the while staring and malevolently smiling at Zeke.

"I do agree," Zeke muttered, worriedly looking toward Hawk and Sarah.

"I have an idea where the next song performance is going to be," Willy indicated, trying to sound business-like. "Of course, we'll have to draw up a contract," Willy specified.

"Quite so, Willy, I agree," modified Zeke. "I'll talk with Hawk."

"Let's talk in private, Zeke," Willy called out as he flew onto a large branch on the oak tree across from the window.

Turning toward Willy's new location, Zeke continued, "You know, Willy, Hawk's popularity has exceeded my expectations. Why he'll be world-famous soon."

Anxiously, Willy responded, "Let's keep this here in Crow City, for now, Zeke. We don't need for Hawk to go to other places, seeing as we're a closely-knit bunch of crows here. And we don't need large crowds from out of town coming here and getting out of hand like what happened at Canary row." Willy was not at Canary Row but had received a report on the rowdy occurrence. "Indeed, nothing escapes my eyes, Zeke."

"Then I'll draw up the contract and have Hawk sign it, Willy," Zeke hastily responded, as he again glanced at Sarah and Hawk. Zeke inwardly mumbled to himself, thinking it was odd that he and Willie were having this long conversation, while Sarah and Hawk were so busy with their own dialogue, laughing and enjoying themselves. He then stopped himself, realizing that he was thinking out loud.

Upon hearing Zeke's words, Willie also turned toward the interacting duo on the window ledge.

"Hmmmm!" mused Willy, staring intently yet in silence at the two, for a few seconds. He finally blurted out, "That sparrow will sing; **contract or no contract**." Quickly he added, "On second thought, I must do things legally, per Crow City's laws. I will draw up the contract, and you, Zeke, will have Hawk sign it. We'll be in touch very soon, Zeke."

With that, Willy gathered up the remaining crows that were on patrol and had now cleared the entire area. Only Hawk and the quartet were left, as the four singers listened determinedly to Hawk and Sarah's conversation.

"I didn't know you were singing about your father, Hawk. What a dreadful thing it was that happened to him," Sarah responded. "It was just dreadful," she again exclaimed, placing her hand over her mouth.

"Yes," Hawk agreed, in a low tone. "I've been trying to find those bad guys who did this horrible act, but somehow, I've ventured into a singing career with Zeke, instead. Whenever I feel that painful hurt in my heart, I just sing the story," Hawk stated.

His response triggered renewed weeping in Sarah, and the quartet as she noted, "Yet you sing so beeeutiful. It's because you truly sing from your heart."

"**And that he does**," called out a powerfully loud, familiar voice. "You're learning to see with your heart, Hawk," the voice went on.

"Malachi!" both Hawk and Sarah rang out in a joyful shout.

"You know him too?" Hawk inquired of Sarah, very pleasantly surprised.

But instead of answering, Sarah asked, "Is it time, Malachi?"

"Time for what?" Hawk probed.

But Malachi remained silent, his golden wings shimmering in the sun, blinding Hawk so powerfully that he had to squint. Hawk had not seen Malachi since the miracle of the musical instruments at the church service with the angels. At this point, Hawk noticed that Malachi's feathers seemed even more luminously radiant with beautiful amber light. He also noticed that Sarah was not squinting.

"No, little one, "Malachi finally interjected to Sarah's question. "It is not the time. But soon it will be." With an authoritative voice now, Malachi continued as he addressed Hawk, "Be wary to follow the right path and stay in the light, Hawk."

Hawk quickly looked up, catching a glimpse of Malachi, whose eyes glistened with sparks of fire, as if he could see right through Hawk.

This being is from out of this world," thought Hawk.

"That's right," Malachi responded to Hawk's thought. "I'm from the third heaven."

Hawk's mouth dropped. "Why, you can read my thoughts," gasped Hawk.

Malachi lifted his huge golden wings and faced south for a few seconds, then flew north, as if responding to a call from a command in the distance; a call that only he could hear.

Hawk and Sarah both turned northward simultaneously, amazed to see a mighty whirlwind coming toward them, twirling round and round a huge cloud with fiery lightning flashes emanating from its midst. Great brightness circled the whirlwind, as the color of amber radiated from amidst the fire. Hawk and Sarah watched Malachi fly directly into it, disappearing from sight.

"Looks like an enormous storm," Georgie pointed out.

"I've _never_ seen a storm like that before," exclaimed Teddy.

The entire quartet was mesmerized by the whirlwind and its grandiose display.

Blinded by the luminous flashes of lightning, the quartet did not see Malachi. Although they did hear the intense conversation between Malachi, Hawk, and Sarah, they were dumbfounded and didn't know what to say.

Chapter Twenty-One
A Peculiar Storm

"Hey, guys, what's with all the flashing lights?" Zeke asked with great interest. "Oh, oh," he interjected, answering his own question. "Looks like a storm is coming," he added, glancing at the fast-approaching whirlwind. He had alighted on the ledge, after having carefully examined the details of Hawk's contract for his next performance.

It was evident at this point that a huge storm was quickly approaching Crow City, though not exactly what Zeke could have imagined. He did notice that Hawk was alone, now. Sarah and Hawk had said their good-byes just in time, before the wind had become as strong as it was at the moment, spinning dirt devils and leaves up in the air. Raindrops began to fall and suddenly the sky became dusky, interspersed with flashes of lightning and loud thunderclaps inundating the blustery

109

atmosphere. The unsettled climate prompted Zeke, Hawk, and the quartet to seek shelter immediately.

The very peculiar and unexpected storm quickly came and went through Crow City, pelting huge raindrops on roofs, roads, and everything in its path. The whirlwind spun around like a prancing ballerina, shaking branches and violently swaying the trees. The brightness of the flashing lightning lit up the shadowy night.

The bird quartet, along with Zeke and Hawk, had found shelter in an abandoned birdhouse of the oak tree across from Sarah's window. Water streamed down the window like tiny rivers. Sarah was worried about her little feathered friends, whom she could no longer see in the dark stormy night. Kneeling on the floor, Sarah clasped her hands together in prayer.

"God, please take care of Hawk and his friends. Amen."

The wind rocked the birdhouse back and forth in a seesaw motion, rocking Zeke to sleep. The quartet, however, Georgie, Lenny, Teddy, and Richey, all huddled tightly together, trembling, not from the cold but the bombastic onslaught of the storm. Each bird released in succession a soft chirp to comfort one another. It appeared like every living thing had taken shelter from this abrupt *peculiar* storm at Crow City.

———

On the other side of town, at James Feed and Seed Store, Paxie nestled under the eaves of the tin roof, above a window. Raindrops descended, sounding like an army of small tin soldiers marching across the roof, making ready for battle.

"I don't think I can take this awful city much longer," Paxie wailed. "*I must find Hawk soon.*" Too exhausted from the ordeal of the night before, and with very little time to eat, Paxie wanted to cry.

Having ended up at James Feed and Seed to inquire about his friend's whereabouts, Paxie nonetheless wondered whether Hawk would still be the same kind of friend he had always been to him, considering his new fame and all.

All the atrocious experiences he had gone through in Crow City, the incessant harassment from the brutal crows and the trampling he suffered at Canary Row, left Paxie feeling very dejected. He still had aches, cuts, and bruises on his face and head from the ordeal. But putting his thoughts aside, Paxie went back to trying to get inside the feed store, realizing it had been shut due to the storm. His only choice now was to wait until the storm passed. His intense weariness easily gave in to sleep. Ah, precious sleep.

Annoyed by Zeke's snoring, Hawk decided to look out the small window of the birdhouse in hopes of seeing Sarah. But the rain was still coming down hard, hindering his view.

Earlier, Zeke had told Hawk about Willy drawing up the singing contract but had not discussed it any further, due to the ominous storm that was approaching. Hawk brooded over the unjust predicament he was in. The more he meditated over this inequitable contract, the more resistant to it he became.

"Why, I can sing for whomever I want, whenever I want," Hawk remarked to himself. "I will do just that," he added more emphatically now, raising his voice. He was fortunate that no one heard him because the quartet members had finally settled down and drifted off to sleep. Zeke also was deep in slumber. His rhythmic snoring moved his head to and fro, one arm up in the air as if holding something in his hand. Hawk gazed at Zeke as he slept. "He's conducting music in his sleep. Oh, brother," mused Hawk.

Zeke dreamed he was at Pigeon Square, conducting delightful music, while the quartet sang spectacularly, wooing the crowd.

"Bravo, bravo!" proclaimed the crowd.

Zeke had his eyes closed, pompously conducting the singers with such ecstatic energy that he failed to see that Hawk was missing until he again opened his eyes. Carefully surveying the crowd, all he could see were the angry crows glaring back at him, but no Hawk. Then Zeke came to an abrupt stop and queried the quartet.

"Where is Hawk?" he demanded.

Answering simultaneously, the foursome responded, "He's singing with Sarah!"

In his sleep still, Zeke yelled out, "Hawk, Hawk, where are youuuuu?"

"Well, if you had opened your eyes, you would have seen that I'm right in front of you, Zeke," replied Hawk loudly, still perturbed at Zeke.

Zeke now opened his eyes and blurted out, "Pigeon Square."

"What?" retorted Hawk.

"We must go back to Pigeon Square," exclaimed Zeke in a loud tone.

Chapter Twenty Two
Return to Pigeon Square

"Pigeon Square?" echoed Hawk in a shocking response to the suggestion. "But why?" he asked abruptly, startling not only the dozing quartet that had finally settled down but himself as well.

"That's where it all started," mumbled Zeke to himself, as he got his backpack ready to go. "Come on then, let's go. There will be plenty of food there, and I'm starving." Thinking he could now persuade Hawk to sign the contract, Zeke added, "Didn't you say your friend, Rex and his friends hang out there sometimes?"

"Yes," responded Hawk, "but what about the *crows*?"

"Oh, not to worry, Hawk; tonight they will be at their annual Crow City Chair meeting held at James Feed and Seed. Everyone will be at Pigeon Square, and it will be just like old times; plus, it will give you another opportunity to display your marvelous talent."

Reluctantly, Hawk agreed.

Lenny, Georgie, Teddy, and Richey were also excited about singing together again and started chirping. Even as they cautiously peeked out the door of the birdhouse to check on the weather, they trembled still from the aftermath of the peculiar storm's bizarre effects. They gathered at the birdhouse door.

Then Georgie pointed out excitedly, "Oh my, Zeke! Look, a double rainbow."

"This is grand," interjected Teddy.

Hawk quickly made his way to the door. To his amazement, a gigantic double rainbow hung suspended against the blue-black sky; a display of purplish hues, bright red and yellow, and emerald green that shone brightly. An overwhelming melancholic feeling tugged at Hawk's heart as a thought from the past crept upon him.

"Paxie!" Hawk announced, tears softly streaming down his cheeks.

———

Paxie awakened from his much-needed rest to the noisy sound of discordant cawing.

"Hey Willy, look, the store's open now," exclaimed Stanley.

"Well it's about time," remarked Willy impatiently.

This second voice alarmed Paxie. No doubt who this was. Paxie had surely had more than his fair share of unpleasant encounters with this fellow. Paxie asked a feathered stranger where James Feed and Seed store was located. He knew Hawk's uncle owned the store in Crow City from past discussions with Hawk. Hoping to find Hawk he headed to the store after the bird concert.

"Oh no, I'll have to hide," Paxie whispered to himself. But Paxie didn't move from under the eaves above the window, trembling at the thought of another unpleasant clash with Willy, himself.

The mob of crows now flew past him, oblivious to Paxie's presence.

The door to the feed store was being held open by James, the store owner, and his two employees – two excessively talkative parrots who happened to be touring Crow City. They had run out of resources and had landed a temporary job at the store. After the last crow was indoors, the door was locked once again and a 'Closed' sign was placed at the window. Paxie shuddered, closing his eyes, as he heard their intermittent boisterous caws and boorish conversation.

"Let this meeting come to order," announced Willy.

"Hey fellows," interrupted Stanley, "wasn't that quite a storm that passed through Crow City?"

"Be quiet, Stanley, there are more important matters to discuss," interjected Jet, who had just been promoted to secretary to Willy.

"Take roll, Jet," demanded Willy.

"What could be more important than this peculiar storm that raced through Crow City?" questioned Stanley.

All this time, Willy glared at Stanley with piercing eyes. Hissing through clenched teeth, he announced, "We're here to discuss a singing contract. Now if you don't mind, I have the floor, Stanley."

Glad to be safe and out of the crows' view, Paxie listened as they argued. He also noticed that the parrots' eyes widened at Willy's uncivil behavior. James, the store owner, however, was not the least bit bothered as he went about his business of taking inventory of the seed and supply.

"These parrots aren't used to such unpleasant behavior, and neither am I," declared Paxie, "I think I'll take a flight and see if I can find something to eat."

Aware that he had to return to talk to James about Hawk's whereabouts, he hesitated. By now, the storm had subsided, allowing Paxie to scavenge for food, as he was running out of the meager food supply he had.

Grabbing his tattered backpack, Paxie looked up at the still dusky sky. To his amazement, a gigantic double rainbow had materialized, demonstrating beautiful, brilliant colors of red, glowing yellow, bluish violet, and emerald green.

Wow, thought Paxie, struck by an overwhelming, mournful feeling that gnawed at his soul. Thoughts of his dad, mom, and siblings invaded his head. Paxie missed his home with its many comforts. But even more than that, he missed the easy and caring way of life he'd had with family.

Crow City was harsh, and survival was the way of life for Paxie, but he was determined to find Hawk.

"I must find Hawk," he whispered, with tears streaming down his cheeks. Then gazing at the rainbow once more, he thought, *A beautiful rainbow amidst a chaotic brutish city.* That city, as he had learned, could be downright dangerous; and now, a friend that seemed so elusive.

——

Sarah woke up refreshed from her nap, singing a song Hawk had taught her. Then, throwing off her covers, she jumped out of bed, humming, *"The early bird gets the worm; the early bird gets the worm. But the late bird gets the dirt!"* She was eager to check on her little feathered friends as she mused, "Oh dear, I hope they're okay. This was such a fierce storm! A very peculiar storm indeed."

As she ran barefoot toward the window, Sarah stubbed her toe on the corner of her bed. Screaming, "Ouch, ouch!" she hopped on one foot. Then, using her hand, she was able to steady herself on the window-sill to look out the window. "Oh goodness gracious; will you look at that gorgeous double rainbow!" she exclaimed excitedly.

"A gift from the Creator," echoed a familiar, author-itative voice behind her.

"Yes, indeed," cried out another equally com-manding voice.

Sarah didn't have to turn around to see who was behind her. The fiery reflections on the window revealed the two angelic visitors, Nahum and Caleb.

"Look at those awesome glowing colors," Sarah announced in ecstatic amazement. Unable to take her eyes off the double rainbows, she added in great delight, "I see vibrant reds, awesome blues, and brilliant yellows. And look at those magnificent emerald colors."

"Like the color of your eyes, Sarah. Who were you talking to just now?" asked the nurse, who had just walked in to give Sarah her lunch.

"Oh, those were my angels, Caleb and Nahum. We were admiring the double rainbows."

"Why that's quite a childish imagination, Sarah," responded the nurse, "but you know, there is a pot of gold at the end of those rainbows."

"Oh Sandy, that is absolutely silly," was Sarah's automatic response. "Do you really believe that?"

Blushing, Nurse Sandy quipped, "Uh, I will go get your medication, now."

Sarah could see Caleb and Nahum grinning. "A pot of gold, she says," Sarah remarked, "and isn't she old enough to know better?" Sarah sat down to eat her lunch in the company of her two angelic visitors.

———

Zeke, Hawk, and the quartet had arrived at Pigeon Square promptly at lunchtime. The air was misty and the clean, sweet fragrance from the rain still lingered in the puddles of water scattered everywhere. The birds had already started feasting on the freely available bread crumbs found on the ground. Soggy as they were, the ravenous birds, upon arriving, eagerly gulped them down. Not only did the feathered community appear on the scene in the aftermath of the storm that struck Crow City, but tourists as well, together with their children. They had come to continue their sightseeing expedition, which the storm had interrupted.

One of the young visitors, Todd, said curiously, "Mom, look at those sparrows *scarfing* down the scraps. Can I get seed for them?"

"No, Todd. Let's go," his mother responded spontaneously. "It looks like this storm may come back again."

Upon hearing this conversation, Zeke looked up and saw the thick black clouds that appeared due north of Pigeon Square, but could not determine if the storm clouds were truly approaching. Not wanting to take any chances, however, Zeke gave out a call.

"Excuse me for interrupting this bounteous banquet of food scraps, folks. I have a treat for you today." He went on to announce, "We have a celebrity among us; a rising star who just made his debut at Canary Row! Please allow me, Zechariah Birdfield as his manager, to introduce to you once again, the Crow City Song Sparrows, featuring the one and only, renowned singing sparrow, Hawk!"

"Why, look! It's Hawk, himself!" a pigeon blared out while munching on breadcrumbs.

"Yes, yes," a dove remarked excitedly. "I recognize him from the bird-fest at Canary Row. What a **voice**!"

Zeke nodded in agreement to the pleasant remarks being made.

"He's one of us!" piped in a sparrow, proudly. "Sing for us, Hawk," he added. "We'd love to hear from you."

A rowdy muttering followed his remarks, from the multitude of birds that had turned up for lunch at Pigeon Square.

Suddenly, a large flock of birds crowded around Hawk, asking for his autograph. Zeke was quite pleased with the way things were rolling.

Perhaps now, Hawk will focus his attention on his music career, instead of on Sarah, thought Zeke. Eager to go on with the show, Zeke interrupted the goings-on, prompting, "There will be more time to meet with Hawk after the show, folks. But now, let's listen to our talented celebrity as he displays his special gift."

Hawk turned his attention to Zeke, who responded, in turn, with a nod for Hawk to commence with the show. In his enthusiasm, Hawk's subtle annoyance at his friend's intrusive request had gone unnoticed. But within himself, Hawk wondered in more than slight agitation, *I came to eat, and now I have to sing for my food again?*

———

Sarah had finished her lunch and was at the window once more, hoping the rainbows were still there. Appearing more faded now, she could still see their display against the still bluish-black stormy sky. She squinted to see the colors more clearly.

Nahum spoke just then. "This grand display of rainbows is a sign for Noah and all humanity, of the graciousness of the Most High, the Creator of all," he expounded.

"It's a promise that stands forever and ever." Caleb's remark echoed throughout the room and down the hall, like thunder.

"Oh dear," a nurse's voice was heard, outside the room. "Was that thunder?"

Sarah turned and glanced at Caleb, as she let out a joyful sound. "Amen to that." Then she instantly turned again to watch the almost completely faded rainbow, and sighed. Her sigh was mimicked by two simultaneously loud sighs from Caleb and Nahum.

Suddenly, a black blur in the distance caught Sarah's attention.

"What in the world is that?" she asked.

No sooner had the last words come out of her mouth than the black blur whizzed past them.

"That was a crow from the crow patrol," Caleb exclaimed in surprise. "It appears he was traveling pretty fast."

"Yes, but not at the speed of light," Nahum pointed out.

"You travel at the speed of light?" Sarah questioned.

"That's why we could see that he was a crow," Caleb clarified.

———

Surprising the quartet, Hawk started to sing a song Sarah taught him. *His eye is on the sparrow...and I know he watches over me.* Hawk sang with such passion, the doves spread their wings and started cooing. The sparrows sighed ecstatically to this acknowledgment of

someone watching over them, and they wept profusely. Others in the feathered crowd wept and some placed their hands over their hearts. Hawk continued singing songs Sarah taught him. The quartet joined in, harmonizing perfectly. Some of the tourists joined in. It just seemed like the right thing to do.

The feathered crowd was awestruck, including Zeke.

"My my," mumbled Zeke. "Sarah indeed has taught him some extraordinary songs." Zeke pondered on plans for the future. "The sky is the limit," he continued, looking up at the sky, "and it won't stop....oh oh, what's that?" Zeke rubbed his eyes and squinted.

The black burr slowed down, took a bird's eye view of Pigeon Square, then sped off. Zeke's jaw dropped. It was a crow. He knew there was only one crow assigned during the crow's meeting to patrol Crow City. He had gambled on the rogue crow not showing up, due to the crows' aggressive behavior toward the patrons and visitors. Store owners had attempted numerous times to chase away the rebel crows without success.

At this point, Zeke, scrambling for ideas to end the performance, looked up at the sky, and blurted out, "Okay, the show's over folks! It's time to scram! Rather... I mean, go." Just then they heard the sound of thunder, to Zeke's contentment. "Yes, indeed. You see, a storm *is* coming," Zeke declared, nervously.

Hawk's fans became very annoyed but had no grounds to protest. Sure enough, the storm was rolling in again.

———

Paxie watched the rainbow until every bit of color had faded from sight.

"I wonder where it disappeared to?" Paxie asked, stretching his neck to look around at the dark clouds and lightning in the distance, approaching from the north. "Oh, gosh! Now I'll have to stay. But I may as well since I have to ask James if he knows where Hawk could be."

Peeking through the window once more, to see if the meeting was over, Paxie observed the birds' fiendish behavior, shuddering at their continuous quarreling over who would get the prime seed. They even tossed bags of feed all over the floor, ripping bags open and scattering the seed all about. He could see that the parrots were fuming, but couldn't voice their opinions because they were only the *hired help*.

Paxie knew from experience not to challenge the crows. It was obvious by James' expression that he had a revelation regarding the matter, but was helpless to dispute their ill-mannered behavior. Submissively, he simply retreated to a corner of the room.

The front door suddenly flew open, slamming abruptly against the wall. Paxie jumped back quickly, shaken by the loud noise. He continued to peek inside.

"Illegal gathering at Pigeon Square. Zeke has a show going on," declared the rogue crow, huffing and puffing. "And that's not all," he went on. "Hawk is singing up a storm."

"A storm?" Stanley interjected, and quickly continued as he looked out the window, "Hey, *fellas*, there's another storm brewing."

"Be quiet, Stanley. This meeting is not officially over," quipped Jet.

"Whaaat?" bellowed Willy, jumping to his feet. "Why, the nerve of these sparrows!"

On hearing Hawk's name mentioned, Paxie listened attentively.

"What do we do with law-breaking sparrows, *fellas*?" asked Willy slyly.

"Put them in jail, I say," responded Jet loudly. "Especially Hawk," he further noted.

"Wait *fellas*," Stanley explained, "he hasn't broken the law. He just won't sign a contract."

"That sounds like a splendid idea, Jet. Crow City County jail just might teach him a lesson," Willy added.

"But, but, Willy, won't that be illegal? Throwing Hawk in the pen for breaking no law?"

"Well, how about *disturbing the peace*?" asked Jet.

"As far as I'm concerned, they are **all** disturbing the peace right now. **Now let's go!** We have a clean-up job to do at Pigeon Square," demanded Willy.

The meeting broke up abruptly. Willy and the gang of crows high-tailed it out the door to dismantle the illegal gathering at Pigeon Square. Paxie quickly jumped out of the way, nearly being trampled on again by the mob of angry crows. Then, making sure they were all gone before entering through the front door, Paxie proceeded with his plan to find Hawk.

James was sweeping the floor, together with the two parrots. The seed was scattered in every direction, even on the parrots' feathers.

"Just look at this mess," exclaimed one of the parrots, called Paco. He continued angrily, "These crows are messy and rude."

"I know! Let's get this cleaned up and go for a flight," the other parrot, Juan said.

James had been aware that they intended to quit. He had been through these situations before. With that in mind, he said to them, "Uh fellows, did I tell you that you had a raise coming?"

With no response, the parrots took their aprons off and headed for the front door, only to bump into Paxie.

When Paxie saw the place, he thought a tornado had hit it. Seed sacks laid open, their content scattered everywhere.

Just then, James called out, "Paco, Juan, come back. We're not done yet."

"Oh yes, we are," stated Paco. They flew out the door in haste.

Paxie continued to survey the damage, all the time mumbling to himself, "My, my, my!"

"Who are you?" demanded James, now at his wit's end.

"My name is Paxie, and I'm looking for your nephew, Hawk!"

Before James could answer, an explosive sound of thunder shook the store, deafening everyone. The thunder rattled the windows and its blustery wind blew the door open, dispersing papers, seed, and dirt every which way, on James' newly swept floor.

Hastening to close the door, James ran to the window to see the rapidly approaching storm. Realizing that there were no longer any crows in view, he gave voice to his thoughts. "How foolish. Those crows could be flying into a horrific storm."

"What?" asked Paxie.

James quickly turned to look straight in Paxie's eyes and noted, "Uh, you didn't hear that from me."

Paxie's instant response was, "I heard they were going to clean up Pigeon Square, and that Hawk is singing there now."

"Ah yes, my famous singing nephew," was James' retort. "They want to put him in jail for not signing a contract," James went on, as he again faced the window. "They won't get very far. This storm will turn them into *feathers*." James snickered.

"Just black feathers!" said Paxie, in jest, restraining laughter, as a loud pounding at the door now interrupted him.

With the booming sounds came some alarmed voices. "Hurry! Let us in!"

James scurried to open the door, to find two dripping wet and shivering parrots, Paco and Juan.

"What happened to you two?" James asked anxiously.

"This blasted storm nearly pulled our feathers out," answered the two employee parrots in gasping spurts.

"Did you see the crows out there?" asked James.

"We saw them from a good distance. They were flying straight into the storm," answered Juan.

Both parrots were now staring curiously at Paxie, wondering who he might be.

Paxie clarified, "Oh, I'm Paxie. I am looking for Hawk. Do you know him?"

"He hangs around a sparrow named Zeke, but do not..." Paco stopped in the middle of his answer.

Paxie suddenly cut in with, "His manager! I saw him at the bird-fest at Canary Row."

"Word has it that Hawk befriended a little girl named Sandy, whom he sings songs to," indicated Paco.He added, "but it may be gossip."

Correcting him, Juan interjected, "I believe her name is Sarah."

"Well, whatever her name is, you won't be going out to find Hawk in this storm, unless you want to be featherless," chortled James. "I'm really bushed now and ready to turn in for the night," James exclaimed with a yawn. "But I do want to welcome you guys back."

Chapter Twenty-Three
The Peculiar Storm Returns

Paco, Juan, and Paxie continued their conversation about Hawk and Zeke's whereabouts.

———

Zeke, Hawk, and the quartet took flight in a rush, narrowly escaping the crows. The rain was beginning to fall at Pigeon Square, and the wind howled fiercely, hurling leaves, debris, and anything not anchored down, forcefully hustling Zeke, Hawk, and the quartet home. They all arrived safely home, although drenched and in shivers. The quartet huddled together, chirping softly, as they instantly fell asleep.

Five minutes after the feathered performers and spectators left the scene, the crows arrived at Pigeon Square.

"Well, this beats all. They all fled the crime scene," proclaimed Jet. "Let's get cracking after them!"

In protest, Willy stammered, "No, no," as he considered the fierce storm. "It's too late, now. We'll deal with this tomorrow. I have an idea." He grinned slyly. "Let's go to Crow City Park instead, *fellas,*" Willy urged in high volume, making Jet jump back.

Some of the crow patrol clean-up crew were gleaning what was left of the lunch buffet: soggy crumbs, seeds, and other edibles. The store owners were peering out the windows.

"What's with all these crows?" asked one of the proprietors.

"I don't know," replied his employee, as he stared at Willy, "but they really are pests. Look at their deplorable behavior," continued the employee, still peeking. "They always seem so aggressive and undisciplined."

"Well, let's close the store early and call it a day before the storm gets worse," declared the owner.

The horde of crows disappeared into the now dusky sky, heading toward Crow City Park, struggling against the rain and wind. Their caw, caw, cawing echoed through the sky, faces set like flint, determined to beat the escalating storm home.

"Feathers is what's we'll be," complained Stanley, while flying close to Jet. "If we don't make it home…"

Jet glared at him a moment, then quickly flew on ahead of him.

The storm had brought everything to a halt at Crow City. Lights were dimming or altogether shutting off, forcing Crow City residents to turn in for the night. Ominous darkness had been cast over the sky, disrupted only by flashes of lightning, creating bizarre shadows on various objects. The winds continued to howl, producing eerie sounds, creaking from the doors along with tapping on the windows.

The quartet fell asleep, exhausted from the day's activities, altogether skipping dinner. Zeke and Hawk munched on seed cakes that one of Hawk's fans had given them.

"You were superb, Hawk," commented Zeke, "Did Sarah teach you those wonderful songs?"

"Uh huh," answered Hawk. "She used to sing in a choir at her church. I will visit her tomorrow," he noted.

Zeke then announced, "Oh, we have practice tomorrow with the quartet. They're also adding new songs to the program."

"What time, Zeke"? Hawk inquired.

"Uh, in the morning, after breakfast," responded Zeke.

"Better get to bed, then," Hawk interjected, not willing to tell Zeke that he had a plan of his own for the next day. He would get up early and visit Sarah before breakfast, knowing she was an early riser, just like him.

———

Sarah had been sound asleep until a bright flash of lightning lit up the sky, followed by a deafening crash of thunder that shook her awake. Alarmed, she jumped up to a sitting position on her bed. The lightning somehow remained in her room, as if suspended in mid-air; flashing, shimmering, twirling amber colors and sparks around a figure that also had appeared in her room. "Malachi!" Sarah exclaimed.

———

Finally reaching their Crow City park destination in the dark hours, the drenched crows, led by Willy, entered their home. It was a huge multi-branched oak tree, which also served as their headquarters. Every crow had his spot; ranking from the best branch, designated for leaders, to the lower branches, for the less wise, less aggressive members.

Breaking the silence, Willy bellowed in a complaint, "Hey, someone's in **my** place!" The darkness made it difficult to see who the stranger could be. "Answer. Speak up," demanded Willy. "Someone, get a light for me," he ordered.

Then a retort was heard, "No need for a light Willy. It's me, Tom."

"Well, pull my feathers! What on earth brings you to Crow City all the way from Hootersville?" petitioned Willy.

"I came ahead to make preparations, and to attend the Crow City annual meeting with Jojo," remarked Tom.

"Jojo?" exclaimed Willy, catching his breath and feeling uneasy at hearing the news. He quickly added, "But I thought Jojo was retired."

Calmly, Tom explained, "Oh, he's back in politics. He heard that Crow City was getting out of control, making all kinds of silly rules, so he sought a commission at Hootersville as mayor, and they sent him here to straighten out the mess."

"Mess?" yelled out Willy, fidgeting with his badge as he talked.

Then Tom continued, "Well, be ready for that meeting with Jojo at lunchtime. He wants everyone there at 12:00 noon sharp, Pigeon Square. I'll see you there."

Quickly, Willy asked, "Wait, where are you going, Tom?"

"I'm going to find an old friend," replied Tom.

"In this weather?" quipped Willy.

"Why yes, Willy. You just need to know how to fly like an eagle." With that, Tom vanished into the darkness. One could hear his singing as he went on his way...
" His eye is on the sparrow and he watches over meeeee."

Everyone in Crow City was fast asleep at this hour. The lights were all out, except for three houses. Sarah was having an intense but pleasant visit with Malachi. Paxie was conversing with Paco and Juan about looking for Hawk.

"We can show you the area where Hawk and Zeke hang out," declared Juan.

"It's a huge five-story house near a gigantic oak tree," added Paco. He continued, "Many people live there that are hurt and need help."

"They call it a hospital where Hawk visits his friend named Sandy," added Juan.

"Sarah," responded Paco. "Her name is Sarah," he persisted. "Hawk sings with her and draws quite a crowd, this is how we know all this information. Hawk is a well-known singer in Crow City."

This was not a new revelation for Paxie since he was at Hawk's singing debut, but it did stir his heart.

———

Willy and the gang of crows were also continuing late into the night. discussing the event that just occurred.

"This is going to ruin our plans, Willy,"were Jet's worried words.

"Yeah, how are we going to arrest Hawk and put him in the cage?" asked Jay, one of the Crow Patrol sergeants.

"*Fellas*, you heard Tom. This is one of the silly rules," Stanley answered.

There was an immediate barrage of insults and scorn from the other crows and loud squawking.

"Fellas, quiet! Stanley can give us some valuable information since we still have one crow on patrol during the meeting with Jojo," remarked Willy. Glaring at poor Stanley, he continued, "Now, what do you know about Hawk's schedule? I know you fraternize with these sparrows as if they were your kind."

"Hawk is an early bird," said Stanley, squirming. "He, uh, he gets up early."

There was a roar of laughter from the horde of crows.

"You're foolish," exclaimed Jet.

"We're all early birds," hollered Willy, a bit agitated. He then ordered Stanley to tell him the details about Hawk's early morning activities.

Stanley pointed out, "Word has it that Hawk visits Sarah before breakfast as I said. He's an early, early bird."

"We will do something about this early early bird," jeered Willy.

"Throw him in the Crow City Cage," remarked Jet.

The crows continued into the wee hours of the morning, contriving a scheme to apprehend Hawk. But now, they had to take into consideration the meeting with Jojo at noontime, all things considered.

———

"I would like to see Hawk one more time," Sarah said, tears streaming from her eyes. "He's a special little sparrow blessed with the amazing gift of singing."

Prompt to respond, Malachi clarified, "Yes indeed, Sarah. The Most High has endowed him with unique singing talent. Furthermore, he will continue to get better and better, as long as he stays on the right path to fulfill his destiny. And you will see Hawk two more times. Although he will have his share of trials, he'll come through without even one of his feathers falling to the ground...this time." Pausing briefly and gazing at Sarah, Malachi went on, "There will come another time in Hawk's near future that will be quite troubling for him."

Her vision intently fixed on Malachi, Sarah noticed that his eyes were fiery, yet sorrowful, as he prophesied this eventful period in Hawk's life. Saddened by the foreboding news, Sarah debated whether to ask Malachi the questions that had entered her mind.

Perceiving her thoughts, Malachi intervened, "It's not for you to know, Sarah, but I must go now. Nahum and Caleb are here." With that, Malachi disappeared instantly into a gloriously bright cloud that exuded lightning flashes from its midst and enveloped his presence.

Turning to Nahum and Caleb, still watery-eyed, Sarah questioned, "Did you guys hear what Malachi said about Hawk?"

In an immediate response, Caleb explained, "Yes, Sarah, we heard because we were here with you, since we never leave your side."

Nahum agreed, "No, we never do." Then, referring to Hawk, he went on, "Hawk is in the Most High's hands."

Caleb then added, "But you sleep peacefully tonight, Sarah."

Those last words seemed to soothe Sarah's mind, and she drifted off to a gentle sleep while listening to the rain tapping gently on the rooftop, resonating like the tick-tock of a clock.

Chapter Twenty-Four
A Home Called Heaven

Hawk woke up early the next morning, with a meticulous plan whirling in his mind. He would skip breakfast, rush over to see Sarah, and get back before Zeke and the quartet woke up. He gingerly tip-toed across the floor and picked up his backpack. Quickly, he checked for his beautiful white feather; a precious memory from his beloved father. He would share this moment with Sarah, today. His eyes began welling as he beheld his father's white feather safely resting in the little box given to him by his mother, Mary.

Suddenly, Hawk heard a stir from the quartet. "Oh no, they're waking up!" he whispered to himself as he stood still and glanced at his sleeping roommates. He swiftly exited out the door, taking his backpack and priceless possession with him—*Dad's white feather.*

The sun was beginning to rise over the mountains, spreading its golden rays through the trees and peeking through windows, vanquishing the obscure shadows from the night before. Alarm clocks resounded throughout the atmosphere, and the clanging of early-scheduled trains was heard as they deposited their overnight cargo. The aroma of sizzling bacon, percolating coffee, and fresh-baked bread inundated the air.

———

Sarah drifted from one fluffy cloud to another, expressing joyful little sounds in her dreams while laughing ecstatically, yet crying simultaneously. She could see the children playing in the clouds, laughing, singing, and enjoying their games. All the children wore brilliant white robes. Angels around them watched the little ones attentively.

Suddenly, a huge golden stairway emerged from the clouds above. Nahum and Caleb also appeared walking down the golden stairs; their faces joyful and radiant with light; their white robes glistening like the noonday sun. Sarah walked up the golden stairs to join the two guardian angels who had been assigned to her on earth.

Nahum smiled, and Caleb reached out his hand to her, saying, "Sarah, you're coming home with us." As Sarah looked upward, she saw Malachi at the top of the golden stairs. He sparkled with glorious brilliance of amber and sapphire blue colors, interspersed with lightning-like flashes, against the pure white clouds.

"Sarah," a small voice said, with a *tap, tap, tap* that was barely audible. *Tap, tap, tap*.

Sarah recognized the sounds.

"Sarah, wake up, it's me, Hawk, are you awake?"

———

"Up, up, up! It's time to go to work," exclaimed James.

Paxie jumped to his feet, rubbed his eyes, and yawned. Paco and Juan were still snoring. They had stayed up late the night before, talking with Paxie about his friend, Hawk, the famous singing sparrow.

Ironically, Paco and Juan used to sing in their country of Brazil. But now they became encouraged about seeking a singing career for themselves, after hearing Hawk sing at Canary Row.

"Are you *fellas* going to show me where Hawk and Zeke hang out?" asked Paxie, quite loudly.

Paco opened one eye and said, "Why not? We would love to meet Hawk."

Juan stirred and placed his foot down on the wooden perch. He had been sleeping with one foot under his wing. "James has errands for us to run in that area," said Juan, drowsy-toned.

"Yes, and here's the list," agreed James. "Get breakfast first. It may be a long day."

Paxie was used to long days in Crow City. He had been looking for Hawk for a long time, but now he would finally find his elusive friend. His eyes brimmed with tears at the thought of it. Oh, how he missed his dear friend. Would Hawk feel the same way, Paxie wondered. As nostalgic thoughts surged in his mind, Paxie remembered their secret hideout at the creek and the double rainbow. He was certain his friend had not and would not forget him.

———

As she jumped out of bed, Sarah squealed loudly, "Hawk! Wait till I tell you the dream I just had."

"And I have something special to show you, too, Sarah," was Hawk's response, as he searched through his backpack.

They were both extremely excited, talking one to another at the same time. Sarah recalled how Malachi had told her she'd see Hawk again only two more times.

———

"Wake up and look sharp," was the command Willy gave the gang of sleepy crows. "What time is it, Jet?" he asked.

Jet exclaimed, "Time to arrest a sparrow named Hawk." The plan was set. Hawk would be apprehended and be confined to the Crow City Cage today, _at the right time_.

"Well start moving like you have a **mission**, Stanley!" blared Willy persistently. "You and Jet, **get going,**" Willy insisted.

"But we haven't even eaten breakfast," Stanley defiantly protested.

"But we haven't eaten breakfast," echoed Willy, mockingly.

Jet jumped in, proclaiming, "We still have time, Willy. Don't sweat it."

"Well all right, then. Just don't miss the train," Willy was careful to note.

"Train? What train?" Stanley asked in much surprise.

"Stanley, could you be that silly?" Jet quickly inquired.

"Yeah, Stanley," piped up another of his peers, named Tim.

Feeling scorned again by his associates, Stanley hung his head low, somewhat accustomed by now to the hostile criticism from his peers a thought entered his mind, _One day I will call the shots_.

"Well, you guys know just what to do," Willy reminded the crows in full volume. "Everyone else, get ready for the meeting with Jojo at Pigeon Square – noon sharp."

———

Describing her dream to her friend, Sarah explained, "Hawk, the golden staircase was beautiful. My angels were there to greet me. They never leave my side, you know. They looked glorious."

Although still searching for the white feather, Hawk stopped Sarah abruptly, with his alarming response: "The golden staircase! Why I've seen it too."

"You have?" Sarah asked, dumbfounded and wide-eyed. "Isn't it **beautiful**? It appeared to have come straight from heaven."

Not knowing what *heaven* meant, Hawk quickly went on, "I saw the golden staircase at a church, as I peered through a window and saw the angels bringing brand new musical instruments, so bright and shiny that the church members were squinting as they stared at them. But what's *heav*—" he started to ask.

Sarah cut in to say, "What did you have to show me, anyway?"

Retrieving his prized possession from his back-pack, Hawk opened the little box and gently picked up his dad's cherished white feather, saying, "This is my father's white feather, Sarah."

"Oh my! how very beautiful," Sarah expressed in a gentle whisper of awe.

Handing his treasure to Sarah, Hawk related, "My mother gave it to me, and I keep it safely in my back-pack, in this little box."

Sarah found herself at a lack of words, a stream of tears escaping from her eyes. Hawk suddenly realized that besides Paxie, whom he greatly admired, he now had another "best friend" in Sarah. He was so deeply touched by Sarah's tears and compassion, it moved him to sing a song:

"Friends, — stick closely by your side.

They'll be there when you beckon. So that in life's worst storm, you won't be shaken.

On sunny days with you they'll walk. You can count on them as good folk.

Real friends stay closer than a brother; always caring for each other."

"That was an awesome song, Hawk," Sara said with a smile, gently holding the white feather in her hand. She then went on in a solemn tone, "Hawk, I'm going home today." Instantly, tears began to run down her cheeks.

Those words caught Hawk by surprise, momentarily leaving him speechless. He finally verbalized, "What do you mean? Do you have another home?"

"I'm going to the most beautiful home imaginable, Hawk! And it's literally *out of this world*," Sarah expounded. "I'm going home to **Heaven.**"

Hawk remembered hearing about *heaven* from Malachi, who had told him he (Malachi himself) was from the third heaven. And Hawk knew that angels come and go from there and that the Most High lived there.

146

With great curiosity, he questioned Sarah, "Can I go there to visit you?"

Amazed by his question, Sarah stated, "Uh, well… yes. I think I will be seeing you in that glorious place."

Unmistakably confused by all this, Hawk desired to ask even more questions, as he meditated on the meaning of Sarah's answer.

Noticing the puzzled look on Hawk's face prompted Sarah to clarify, "Oh, don't worry, Hawk, we will certainly see each other again. After all, we are *"Best Friends" forever*."

A voice from the hall was heard addressing Sarah, "Here's your breakfast, Sarah."

"Hawk, I have to go now. Here's your father's white feather," Sarah stated as she tenderly handed the feather back to her friend.

"Breakfast. Oh no. I'd better go too. Zeke and the quartet may be looking for me soon," Hawk burst out, nestling the feather back in its box.

Grabbing the backpack, Hawk secured the box in its place and said his farewell to Sarah, "I'll see you soon, Sarah. I'd better take the shortcut home."

I will see you sometime later today, Hawk," said Sarah, recalling what Malachi had told her about seeing Hawk two more times.

Chapter Twenty-Five
Hawk Gets Arrested

Hawk sensed something different in the air today, though he could not pinpoint it. He sensed something portentous was about to occur.

Finding the shortcut home, Hawk was elated that he would be able to see Sarah later that same day.

I will surely ask her where heaven is, next time, Hawk thought, *so I can come to visit her.* He sounded reassured about seeing her again, soon.

———

Jet and Stanley quickly finished breakfast after being shoved out the door by Willy, thus launching the two crows onto their *mission*.

"We'll just tell him that he is to be taken into custody for questioning," declared Jet, speaking of Hawk.

"Oh, that's good," remarked Stanley. "That way, Hawk will have a chance to explain himself," commented Stanley.

In assertion, Jet emphasized, "Just be sure to follow my orders, or uh, Willy's orders, that is." With his next breath, Jet stated, "Oh look. There he is now, up ahead."

"Let's just talk to him, Jet," stressed Stanley.

Stanley yelled at Hawk, "We need to have a word with you, Hawk, follow us to Crow City Park. It's just going to be a quick talk."

Hawk turned around to see the two crows chasing after him were Stanley and Jet. Contemplating the situation, Hawk said, "I may not get away this time." Reluctantly, Hawk agreed to follow Stanley and Jet.

Hawk and the two crows flew toward Crow City Park, where Crow City Jail was situated. Hawk was unaware of the crow's devious plans.

I wonder what they want to talk to me about, he thought.

Moments later the two crows and the famous singing sparrow landed at Crow City Jail.

———

"Where's Hawk?" demanded Zeke.

"We don't know," replied Georgie.

"Did he leave a note?" asked Teddy.

"Maybe he went out to look for food," Lenny declared pensively.

"There's plenty of food, here," remarked Zeke rather annoyed. He added, "I bet I know where he's at." Suddenly there was a knock at the door.

"Maybe it's him," Georgie stated questioningly.

"Why would he knock?" was Teddy's next question, followed by Zeke's convinced reply, "He wouldn't."

He reached the door to open it, only to encounter two large parrots and the sparrow that accompanied them. Surprisingly, no one said a word as Zeke closed the door and went back to discussing Hawk's disappearance.

Well, well, well, if it isn't the famous singing sparrow," declared Willy with a sarcastic smirk, referring to Hawk. "Good job, you two," he stated, looking directly at Stanley and Jet and instructing, "Now put this incorrigible sparrow in the cage."

Stanley hesitated. Tim stepped in, shoving Stanley out of the way as Stanley protested. "But I thought we were just going to talk to him!" remarked Stanley, perplexed, as Jet and Tim seized Hawk swiftly and thrust him gruffly into the cage.

Stunned with shock, Hawk didn't even open his mouth to speak. Finding himself outnumbered by the Crow Patrol surrounding him, Hawk understood all too well he was hardly in a position to protest his captors' brutal behavior toward him.

"Give me that backpack," demanded Jet.

"No," protested Hawk fiercely at Jet's demand. "It is mine."

"That backpack needs to be confiscated!" responded Jet, forcefully grabbing the backpack from Hawk's possession. Examining the pouch's contents, Jet declared, "Well, look at what we have here. A white feather." Mockingly handing the feather to his comrade, Jet said, "This feather would look good in your hat, Stanley."

"Noooo!" screamed out Hawk in aggressive desperation. "That feather belonged to my father, who died. Give it back to me."

"Okay, knock it off!" Willy demanded, "Jet, put that feather down and let's get going right now. Jojo is expecting us at Pigeon Square, soon."

At that moment, Stanley queried, "Hey, Willie, won't JoJo object to our throwing Hawk into the cage?"

"Not if we don't tell him," Willy responded craftily, attempting to control his displeasure at Stanley's remark.

"But Stanley will blab," Jet quickly pointed out.

"Stanley will be staying here to guard the prisoner," Willy announced.

Jet started to protest, but Willy instantly raised his hand in opposition, stating, "Jojo wants every one of us who's 'relevant' to be there at this gathering! So let us go **now**." Then he turned quickly around to face

Hawk, saying, "We'll deal with you later, sparrow. And Stanley, you watch your step. This sparrow better, be in this cage when I return."

"Yeah, sparrow," mocked Jet in agreement.

———

Again, another knock was heard, to which Zeke responded. As he opened the door, Zeke was surprised to find the same two parrots from before and a sparrow. He asked, more irritated than interested, "Yes... what do you want?"

"We are looking for Hawk," Paxie responded quickly, not wanting the door to close again.

"Oh do come in," Zeke said invitingly. "We are looking for him too."

The little sparrow stepped into the middle of the room and introduced himself. "My name is Paxie, and these two are Paco and Juan." The parrots nodded.

It had become extremely crowded in the small birdhouse. The two large parrots occupied most of the space, and never having seen such huge, peculiar birds before, the quartet of sparrows could only stare, wide-eyed.

Addressing Paxie, Zeke asked, "Aren't you Hawk's buddy from Meadowlarksville?"

"Yes, I am," Paxie affirmed. "Where is Hawk? Where can I find him, please?" Paxie asked, frantic to see his dear best friend.

Having endured great hardship in his prolonged time of searching for his friend, Paxie could scarcely control his emotions any longer. Believing that he might be at the end of a long road was almost more than he could bear. He unreservedly burst into tears.

"We don't know where Hawk is," the quartet stated in unison. They too were overcome with emotion at Paxie's obvious brokenness over his friend and wept. Even Zeke was touched by empathy as he witnessed everyone expressing their concern and intimate bond of friendship for their friend, Hawk.

"He may be at Sarah's," Zeke offered, hoping this would be a helpful suggestion, even as he blew his nose.

"That's probably the most likely place. Let's go find out," Paxie cried out impatiently. With that, the parrots were the first out the door, followed by Zeke, Paxie, and the "weepy" quartet.

They replied in unison, "Let's all of us find Hawk for him." Everyone said "amen," to that.

Chapter Twenty-Six
Desperately Seeking Hawk

Sarah found it unusual to see two large Brazilian parrots parked at her window ledge, together with six sparrows.

"They're beautiful," she exclaimed. "Look at those red and green feathers. I wonder where they came from." Catching herself, she thought, *Wait a minute! I recognize those sparrows. They're Hawk's friends, Zeke, and the quartet; the other one, I don't know.*

"The other one is Paxie," interjected Caleb. "He's looking for Hawk."

"They are all looking for Hawk," Nahum emphasized.

"Oh, dear," Sarah noted, "He was here early this morning. But where could he be now?" she declared loudly, a worried expression very vivid on her face.

"Hawk will be all right. He's at the Crow City Cage," confirmed Caleb.

"Well, I will go and get him out," Sarah declared without hesitation.

"No. You have an appointment with the Most High, today. But you will see Hawk one more time, Sarah," was Nahum's admonition to her.

"Remember that this has already been predestined, Sarah," declared Caleb.

"Seeing my little friend one more time will be a blessing," said Sarah, contemplating the song he had taught her this very day. "I'll be so grateful," she stressed, as tears overflowed from her eyes. "We'll sing together one last time. How glorious," she noted, whisper-like.

"He's not here, Zeke!" Paxie yelled out.

"Well, where could he be?" asked Zeke, puzzled about his friend Hawk.

"James Feed and Seed," remarked Paxie, reflectively, and hurriedly continued. "When I was at the store, I overheard the crows threatening to put Hawk in the Crow City Cage. That's where he's at," he affirmed in jubilation.

"Let's go get him," Zeke proposed anxiously, recalling the very unpleasant experience he had encountered there when he too was so forcefully housed at the Crow City Cage AKA Crow City Jail.

"Wait, guys," Paco jumped in. "We need to have a plan for this before we go there. First, we need to try to see him, without risking anyone seeing us, or we could all end up in the cage, ourselves," he added with a shudder.

The quartet shuddered and huddled closer together.

———

At Crow City Jail, Stanley decided to talk with Hawk.

"It's not so bad, Hawk," Stanley explained. "Would you like a book to read?"

Very discouraged, Hawk responded, "Can I just have my backpack now, with the white feather?"

"Well, I don't know…." Stanly answered nervously. "Willy might get his beak tweaked."

"But it's my father's white feather, and it's all I have of him now that he's gone," pleaded Hawk.

Stanley, the "softy," found himself saying, "Oh, all right. I see no harm, here." Stanley picked up the backpack and gave it to Hawk, saying, "Here you go. But can I please just touch the white feather?"

Hawk reached for his backpack. Glad to have it in his possession, he cautiously took out his father's treasured gift, and carefully extended it to his captor. Stanley took the feather with gentleness, touching it softly. Trying unsuccessfully to clear his throat, Stanley was unable to express his gratitude at Hawk's gesture. But the tears he fought hard to conceal said it all. Handing the white feather back to Hawk Stanley cleared his throat and said, "He must've been quite a sparrow."

———

Meanwhile, the feathered liberators, all eight of them, arrived at Crow City Jail, landing on some high window ledges.

"There he is," whispered Paxie, pointing at Hawk.

"Hey, I thought I heard James saying that he and Stanley go way back," noted Paco.

"Shhh, they will hear us," whispered Juan, adding, "They were in some kind of Bird Peace Corps together."

"I bet James can talk to him," exclaimed Paco.

"Go see if he can help us," requested Zeke.

"On my way," responded Paco, rather noisy.

This started a wave of shushes amongst the rest of the feathered comrades. Paxie was dumbfounded.

Feeling helpless, he whispered, "Be brave, Hawk, we will get you out."

This started a soft whimpering amongst the quartet.

———

Paco rushed through the front door of James' Feed And Seed, shouting, "**Hawk got thrown into the Crow City Jail and**...." Paco stopped cold in the middle of his excessively loud statement when he realized how surprised he was to see a crow having lunch with James. "Oh, I didn't realize you had company," he sheepishly said apologetically.

"This is Tom, Paco," answered James. "We knew each other years ago when we were in the Bird Peace Corps together."

"Howdy do!" Tom greeted, nodding his head.

"Oh, so you also go back a long way, just as Stanley does, huh?" inquired Paco.

"Yes, indeed," agreed James with a prideful grin, then quickly asked, "Did I hear you say Hawk was thrown in the Cage?"

Staring at James now, Paco uttered, "Zeke and Paxie want you to come and talk to Stanley, hoping Hawk can be released into your custody."

At this point, Tom cut in, saying, "Well, fellas, it's time for me to go. JoJo will be at Pigeon Square any moment now." Then he added, "Oh, and if you get Hawk out of the cage, I suggest he and his buddies high-tail it out of Crow City **instantaneously.** And with all due respect, JoJo may not be able to control a mob of angry crows. And they will be angry."

"That's an affirmative, Tom," declared James. "See ya."

"Yeah. See ya next time around. I'll go back to Hootersville after the meeting – oh, look, you have a customer." As quickly as Tom flew out, in flew a sparrow named Zelda.

Jojo arrived at noon sharp. He called the meeting to order and afterward took a roll call. To start up the meeting, Jojo announced, "The first thing on the agenda is to discuss some of these silly laws." His comment stirred up a loud murmuring amongst everyone.

"All right, everyone," demanded Willy. "Let's have quiet now. We're going to go through every one of these laws and explain why we need them."

Next, Jojo asked, "Incidentally, do you have this month's census?"

Willy's response was, "No, Jet forgot to bring it."

Confounded, Jet remarked, "Willy didn't instruct me to bring it."

Furiously, Willy retorted, "Well, I'm instructing you, **now. Go get the census**."

Jet flew off in a hurried fury.

———

"I wonder what's taking them so long?" Paxie asked impatiently.

"James is across town, Paxie," clarified Zeke.

"Well, I hope he can help," Paxie stated in a dismal tone.

"Me too," Juan noted nervously.

"He seems to be okay for now," Zeke said with certainty, as he stared intently into the window. "They're playing cards."

The quartet didn't so much as make a peep while peeking into the ghastly cage, which made them shake with fear.

———

Across town at James' Feed And Seed Store, James was about to lock up when an unexpected visitor walked in.

"May I help you, ma'am?" James asked the sparrow that had entered when Tom exited.

"My name is Zelda, and I'm looking for Zeke," responded the ladybird.

"Oh, are you his mother?" James asked.

"Why yes, how did you know?" was Zelda's response.

"There is a strong resemblance," James stated.

"I agree," Paco intervened. "But we'd better get going. They're waiting for us at the cage."

"Oh, dear," Zelda nervously shouted out. "Is Zeke in the cage, again?"

"No, ma'am," Paco cried out quickly. "He is trying to help a friend get out."

"Well, in that case, I'm going with you," exclaimed Zelda.

"Ma'am, this is not a place for ladybirds," Paco declared.

"Oh, but I insist," protested Zelda, who refused to be persuaded by the huge, brightly colored parrot.

James promptly hung up the "Store Closed" sign on the door and locked it, heading rapidly toward the cage with Paco and Zelda who were still conversing about Zelda going with them to the Cage.

James, on the other hand, was thinking about Hawk and his mother, Mary. "I must help Hawk out of this mess," he deliberated. Mary would be devastated if she should lose Hawk, after the tragic loss of Hawk's father.

Chapter Twenty-Seven
Hawk Gets Released

eanwhile, Jet grumbled as he busily searched for the census sheet. He was tossing papers around and kicking boxes filled with files, as he disturbingly complained to himself, "I could care less about this census!" Having arrived at Crow City Park Patrol Headquarters, he was furious that Willy had blamed him for the census report.

"I should be the chief of the Crow City Patrol," continued Jet, irately expressing his dissatisfaction to himself. "I can do just as good a job as he can." By now, Jet had convinced himself that he wasn't going to find the document when out of the blue, he discovered it and laughed in relief. "Found it. Now I can scram."

———

"Look, there's James, Paco, **and Mother**!" declared Zeke, looking up at the feathered troop that soon landed beside him.

After the happy greetings of the group, Paxie went back to business, stating, "Shush. We're too noisy."

"Oh, don't worry, Paxie," Zeke said assuredly. "James will go and speak to Stanley right away, and Hawk will be free in no time."

Subsequently, James did just that.

As he turned to his mother, Zeke asked in wonder, "Mother, what are you doing here?"

Zelda, who was staring at the quartet, responded, "I miss you, Zeke, I came to see if you're okay."

Looking at the quartet Zeke explained, "I am the choirmaster of the Crow City Sparrows, Mother, and this is the singing quartet. Their lead singer is Hawk, but he is in the Crow City Cage at this moment."

"Not anymore," proclaimed Paxie with exuberance. "And here comes James and Hawk, himself."

Stanley was escorting James and Hawk out the front door, as he simultaneously spoke to James saying, "Don't forget our plan, James."

"And what plan would that be?" Paco inquired with great interest.

"Oh, Stanley doesn't know how Hawk escaped," James responded. "I guess Hawk is just a smart cookie!" he replied while winking at Hawk, and saying to him, "I believe you have a friend here who's been looking for you!"

James pointed at Paxie, who gave out a thunderous acclaim, "**Hawk**! Boy, am I glad to see you! Are you okay?"

"Yep, I am now. Thanks to my uncle," Hawk stated with joy. "But I missed you a lot, Paxie."

The two buddies hugged each other as they wept with happiness.

Everyone present began laughing and rejoicing as tears of joy flowed freely among the feathered participants, creating a wave of jubilation. Even Paco and Juan were caught up in the hugging and weeping episode, as were Zeke and his mother and the entire quartet.

The only one who wasn't crying was James. However, he had a dire warning to share with all, stating, "Hawk and Paxie need to leave Crow City immediately."

Shocked at his uncle's abrupt announcement, Hawk asked with a loud tone, "**Now**?"

"Yes, that was the agreement that Stanley and I made. I've seen the crows angry before when someone escaped from the cage. They don't like it one bit."

Stanley had just walked outside to say good-bye. "Willy will explode, you all don't want to be here, so leave now, Hawk. You too, Paxie."

"It's afternoon and they will be finished with their meeting soon," added James.

"But JoJo's back," hollered Zeke.

"Son, that won't stop an angry mob of crows," James said with concern. "Stay away. At least for a season," James advised the group.

"That will give us time to catch up on things, son," commented Zeke's mother to her newly found son.

"Yes, and we still have the quartet, don't we?" asked Zeke, looking at the boohooing foursome.

They all shook their heads in accord. Paco and Juan, who had been silent, offered to help Zeke and the quartet.

"We would love to help out the singing group, Zeke," stated Paco. Juan nodded yes and gave Zeke a thumbs up.

The last of their farewells were said with sadness, as Zeke hugged Hawk and confidently said, "This will only be for a season," hoping this would reassure Hawk. And to Paxie, Zeke said sincerely, "Nice meeting you, Paxie."

"Hawk, you and Paxie better get going," Juan admonished, as one of his friends made him aware that a crow was coming right out of Crow City Park.

———

It was long past the noon hour when Hawk and Paxie packed their belongings for the long trek home. As the two prepared to make their exit out of the horrid

City of the Crows, Hawk suddenly remembered with alarm, "I have to say good-bye to Sarah."

But Paxie reminded him immediately, "Hawk, Juan said one of his friends spotted a crow. Remember?"

"I know," Hawk stated. "But I still have to say good-bye to Sarah. She's going home today," stressed Hawk.

Recognizing that his friend could be pretty stubborn, Paxie agreed, "Oh, all right. Let's make this quick, though."

Elated beyond words, Hawk flew rapidly toward Sarah's place, as Paxie trailed behind him.

"Wait for meee!" yelled Paxie, huffing for breath.

"Huh? What was that?" Jet asked loudly. "Maybe I'm seeing things. I thought I saw two sparrows whizzing by, and one looked like Hawk. I better check this out." Upon checking, Jet confirmed what he had seen – It **was** Hawk and another sparrow. Putting two and two together, Jet surmised, "Hawk probably broke out of the cage, with the help of his friend Zeke." I must warn the Crow Patrol at once." He made his way in 'express' flight straight to Pigeon Square.

Hawk was the first to arrive at Sarah's abode and perched himself on her window ledge. Paxie followed not much later, panting hard, but gasping, stated, "You go say good-bye to Sarah, Hawk. I'll keep an eye out for the crows." *Gasp.* "Then say good-bye for me also, but **hurry,** Hawk!"

Chapter Twenty-Eight
A Glorious Homecoming

Hawk scooted over on the window ledge, just in time to see the glorious heavenly display of the golden staircase as it descended out of the clouds. It was brilliant like the sun, with cascading waves of light emitting from it. Angels in attendance lined up along each side of the stairs, standing on each step.

Nahum and Caleb were escorting Sarah up the stairs. Each angel bowed his head as the glorious trio passed by. An aroma of rose petals was sweetly present in the air. His eyes fixed on the scene, Hawk could hear the beautiful music that filled the atmosphere, along with the thousands of voices that sang in perfect harmony. Sarah, dressed in a flowing sparkling white gown, stepped easily in perfect cadence with her two guardian angels. Her shoes, also sparkling white, matched the elegance of her gown On her head was a gorgeous diadem of flowers.

As they reached the top of the stairs, Sarah saw Malachi; waves of glory and brilliant light all over him. Hawk was able to see him say something to Sarah, as she then turned around and saw Hawk for the last time.

"She looks like a princess!" Hawk said to himself, astounded by it all. Sarah waved at that moment and threw kisses at her tiny sparrow friend – a friend she had delighted in, those last few weeks on earth. Never would she forget him. She mouthed to him in silence, "I will see you again, Hawk, my little buddy."

Amazingly, Hawk could read her lips. He knew deep in his heart he would one day see her again. In one unexpected moment, the golden stairs, the clouds, together with the angels and Sarah, herself, all disappeared.

"Heaven," said Hawk with great amazement, yet peacefully. "She went to heaven." Quietly now, Hawk wondered if he, too, would one day go to this beautiful heaven. And if so, how would he get there?

What he heard next startled him.

"Oh, oh. Incoming!" It was Paxie, screeching as loud as he could, "Hawk! Let's go now!"

Chapter Twenty-Nine
The Great Escape and Crow Anarchy

"There they are," Jet announced with a booming scream. The covetous crow who had always wanted Willy's leadership position had scrambled in a flash to the meeting at Pigeon Square to alert the Crow Patrol. Chaos quickly ensued, and the meeting deteriorated. As a result of this turn of events, JoJo consequently lost all control of the meeting. Never would he have expected the crow anarchy that arose from the crows and their soon-to-be-fired leader, Willy. The hostile crows speedily took to the skies en route to the prisoner sparrow, now escaped.

Hawk's solemn thoughts of Sarah suddenly turned to horror as he heard the familiar cawing of the raucous crows in the distant sky. As he gazed at the sky, Hawk could see the furious crows approaching at lightning-fast speed directly toward the sparrows. To Hawk, this was déjà vu all over again.

Quivering at the prospect, Hawk vividly remembered when he and his friend, Paxie, had been chased by a pack of angry crows at Scarecrow Park.

"They're coming fast and furious at us, Hawk," Paxie yelled in alarm.

"Let's elude this pack, Paxie. I think I know where we can hide," yelled Hawk.

To Paxie, the idea of escaping their vengeful enemies seemed impossible, considering the insurmountable odds against them.

"Come on, Paxie, follow me."

By now, the crows were rapidly gaining momentum, just yards behind the two sparrow buddies. Paxie could hear their hostile threats.

"We will quash you yet. We will trap you in the cage forever!"

Although Hawk and Paxie rapidly increased their velocity, the villains seemed to be catching up to them with equal acceleration and intense aggression.

"Hey, guys, we've got 'em!" screeched Jet to his demon-like pack.

"**Not so fast**," screamed a voice that resounded through the sky. It was Malachi, spreading his enormous wings between the antagonist crows and the fleeing sparrow amigos. Flashes of lightning and golden amber lights surged from his wings, blinding the approaching pursuers.

"Hey, I can't see!" screamed Jet in panic and confusion.

"Neither can I," echoed another, followed by increasing alarm and cries of, "What's going on, here?" and "Wait a minute. Hey, watch where you're going. Careful, there!"

They were all colliding into one another, as extremely bright lightning originating from Malachi blinded their eyes.

In a quandary about what was taking place, both Paxie and Hawk began to slow their pace down. Not only were they anxiously curious about the goings-on, but they were also almost completely out of breath. They witnessed the non-stop flashing of lightning and heard thudding sounds as the crows blindly clashed repeatedly into one another, again and again.

Wanting to see this strange occurrence with the noises and bright lights, Hawk turned around and saw Malachi. His majestic, beautiful golden wings shimmered in the sky as the angelic being triumphantly soared through the sky until the canopy of brilliant clouds enveloped him.

Trying to make a landing and escape their blind frenzy, the mob of crows only continued to collide with one another.

Tired of the turmoil, Jet yelled in desperation, not knowing to whom, "Ouch! Watch where you're going."

"I can't see where I'm going either!" Tim cried in angry frustration.

"Paxie, now's our chance to break away from this swarm of maniac crows," bellowed Hawk. "Look, there's a forest up ahead. Let's scram over there to hide," said Hawk, greatly relieved at the prospect.

"I desperately need a rest. I'm all out of breath," responded Paxie.

"Me too," cried out Hawk.

In their haste, they swiftly entered the dense forest where Hawk and Paxie continued to fly deeper into the woods, to distance themselves from the predator crows. Finally, they were able to land on a pine tree branch, where Paxie thought they would find safety.

As they heavily perched themselves, finally, Paxie suggested, "Let's stay quiet here, Hawk, and keep a careful eye out for the crows. Although I can't hear them anymore," he said, relieved. "What do you think happened to them!" asked Paxie, still breathing heavily. "I saw flashes of lightning and bright lights. Next thing I knew, they were all running into each other as if they had gone blind or mad."

"Malachi!" exclaimed Hawk.

Who?" asked Paxie.

"I'll explain it to you later, Paxie," replied Hawk. "For now, let's just rest. But I am so happy to see you, Paxie," Hawk said joyfully.

"I've been looking for you for a long time Hawk," exclaimed Paxie.

With their tension easing steadily, the sparrow buddies embraced, teary-eyed but happy to have one another. Shortly after, however, their intense exhaustion took over, and the two weary pals were drifting into a deep slumber. Before that, Hawk emotionally summarized his short time in Crow City, recalling his mission for being there had not been accomplished. He hadn't found the two bullies who killed his father and wondered if he ever would. However, he was still determined.

Hawk and Paxie both woke up after a long nap, at the sound of the pleasant melodies the myriad of forest birds sang. Their music was so enchanting and joyful, compared to the crows' piercing cawing.

There were many other beautiful sounds in this contrastingly peaceful sanctuary. The gurgling of rushing waters whirling over the creek's rocks nearby only emphasized the variety of delightful forest sounds. The wind that blew softly on the treetops created a tranquil atmosphere for the two sparrows after their traumatic experience.

"I've never seen a place like this before," remarked Paxie. "Have you, Hawk?"

As Hawk considered the question, he continued looking about, as if he was searching for someone or something, before answering, "I'm not sure, Paxie, but I feel as if I was here before."

Puzzled at his friend's strange reply, Paxie commented, "You're probably tired, Hawk. After all, you were locked up in that horrible cage."

Hawk shuddered at the thought of the distressing experience and quickly changed the subject. "Look at those lovely large brown animals with huge eyes." Hawk was looking at the deer strolling through the trees; their adorable offspring, the fawns, skipping at their parents' side. Rabbits also scurried through the forest, chasing one another; squirrels scurried along as if they had an appointment to keep, stopping only occasionally to sniff the air, keeping a vigilant watch for two cagey foxes they had spotted earlier, lapping water from the creek.

This serene environment was different than any Paxie had ever seen. "What could go wrong here?"

Hawk, however, was still reflecting as to where he could have encountered this scenario before.

Paxie was amazed at the many aromatic fragrances that permeated this 'heavenly' place. He inhaled deeply the widespread aroma of wildflowers that infiltrated the air. The sweet scents of pine and honey saturated the cool forest air, as Paxie relished this newfound forest ambiance. The enchanting fragrances and tranquility of the forest soon captivated Hawk. He sighed.

"Well, I thought I was here before; but maybe not... " Hawk took a momentary deep breath to enjoy his surroundings, but instead inhaled a pungent odor of smoke. His thoughts instantly accelerated at one hundred miles an hour, and he was aware of a faint sound of thunder in the distance. He noticed that the animals, large and small, stood in a frozen position for a brief moment – and then, he **remembered**.

The sound of thunder was the sound of the feet and hooves of animals running through the forest and pounding its floor. The tension in the atmosphere hurriedly turned to an overwhelming fear that filled the whole forest.

Astounded by it all, Paxie cried out desperately, "Hawk, what is happening?"

The odor of smoke was extremely powerful now, and Hawk and Paxie were seeing before them a massive exodus of animals fleeing for the lives.

The smoke, the fire, everything about the forest seemed very surreal to Hawk. He could scarcely believe that this was happening *again*. The last time, this event had occurred in a dream. This time, however, **it was real.** Would it happen the same way it had in his dream? Would the lion named Judah, with six wings, appear? Hawk felt the anguish of Paxie's presence caught up in this inferno. Hawk was deeply mystified.

Knowing he had to act quickly, he shouted, "Come on, Paxie, let's get out of here!"

To be continued.

CPSIA information can be obtained
at www.ICGtesting.com
Printed in the USA
BVHW041321180621
609826BV00003B/414